ANA
MENÉNDEZ

In Cuba I Was a German Shepherd

Grove Press
New York

Published simultaneously in Canada
Printed in the United States of America

"In Cuba I Was a German Shepherd" originally appeared in *Zoetrope: All-Story*.

"Amor de Loca Juventud" by Rafael Ortiz. Copyright © 1997 by Peer International Corporation. International Copyright Secured. All Rights Reserved. Used by Permission.

FIRST EDITION

Library of Congress Cataloging-in-Publication Data
Menéndez, Ana.
  In Cuba I was a German shepherd / Ana Menéndez.
     p. cm.
  ISBN 0-8021-1688-4
    1. Miami (Fla.)—Fiction.   2. Cuban Americans—Fiction.   3. Cuba—Social life and customs—Fiction.   I. Title.
  PS3563.E514 I5 2001
  813'.6—dc21   00-067187

Grove Press
841 Broadway
New York, NY 10003

01 02 03 04   10 9 8 7 6 5 4 3 2 1

For my parents
and for Dexter

Contents

In Cuba I Was a German Shepherd

The park where the four men gathered was small. Before the city put it on its tourist maps, it was just a fenced rectangle of space that people missed on the way to their office jobs. The men came each morning to sit under the shifting shade of a banyan tree, and sometimes the way the wind moved through the leaves reminded them of home.

One man carried a box of plastic dominos. His name was Máximo, and because he was a small man his grandiose name had inspired much amusement all his life. He liked to say that over the years he'd learned a thing or two about the physics of laughter and his friends took that to mean good humor could make a big man out of anyone. Now Máximo waited for the others to sit before turning the dominos out on the table. Judging the men to be in good spirits, he cleared his throat and began to tell the joke he had prepared for the day.

"So Bill Clinton dies in office and they freeze his body."

Antonio leaned back in his chair and let out a sigh. "Here we go."

Máximo caught a roll of the eyes and almost grew annoyed. But he smiled. "It gets better."

He scraped the dominos in two wide circles across the table, then continued.

"Okay, so they freeze his body and when we get the technology to unfreeze him, he wakes up in the year 2105."

"Two thousand one hundred and five, eh?"

"Very good," Máximo said. "Anyway, he's curious about what's happened to the world all this time, so he goes up to a Jewish fellow and he says, 'So, how are things in the Middle East?' The guy replies, 'Oh wonderful, wonderful, everything is like heaven. Everybody gets along now.' This makes Clinton smile, right?"

The men stopped shuffling and dragged their pieces across the table and waited for Máximo to finish.

"Next he goes up to an Irishman and he says, 'So how are things over there in Northern Ireland now?' The guy says, 'Northern? It's one Ireland now and we all live in peace.' Clinton is extremely pleased at this point, right? So he does that biting thing with his lip."

Máximo stopped to demonstrate and Raúl and Carlos slapped their hands on the domino table and laughed. Máximo paused. Even Antonio had to smile. Máximo loved this moment when the men were warming to the joke and he still kept the punch line close to himself like a secret.

"So, okay," Máximo continued, "Clinton goes up to a Cuban fellow and says, 'Compadre, how are things in Cuba these days?' The guy looks at Clinton and he says to the president, 'Let me tell you, my friend, I can feel it in my bones. Any day now Castro's gonna fall.'"

Máximo tucked his head into his neck and smiled. Carlos slapped him on the back and laughed.

"That's a good one, sure is," he said. "I like that one."

"Funny," Antonio said, nodding as he set up his pieces.

"Yes, funny," Raúl said. After chuckling for another moment, he added, "But old."

"What do you mean old?" Antonio said, then he turned to Carlos. "What are you looking at?"

Carlos stopped laughing.

"It's not old," Máximo said. "I just made it up."

"I'm telling you, professor, it's an old one," Raúl said. "I heard it when Reagan was president."

Máximo looked at Raúl, but didn't say anything. He pulled the double nine from his row and laid it in the middle of the table, but the thud he intended was lost in the horns and curses of morning traffic on Eighth Street.

~

Raúl and Máximo had lived on the same El Vedado street in Havana for fifteen years before the revolution. Raúl had been a government accountant and Máximo a professor at the University, two blocks from his home on L Street. They weren't close friends, but friendly still in that way of people who come from the same place and think they already know the important things about one another.

Máximo was one of the first to leave L Street, boarding a plane for Miami on the eve of the first of January 1961, exactly two years after Batista had done the same. For reasons he told himself he could no longer remember, he said good-bye to no one. He was thirty-six years old then, already balding, with a wife and two young daughters whose names he tended to confuse. He left behind the row house of long shiny windows, the piano, the mahogany furniture, and the pension he thought he'd return to in two years' time. Three if things were as serious as they said.

In Miami, Máximo tried driving a taxi, but the streets were a web of foreign names and winding curves that could one day lead to glitter and another to the hollow end of a pistol. His Spanish and his University of Havana credentials meant nothing here. And he was too old to cut sugarcane with the younger men who began arriving in the spring of 1961. But the men gave Máximo an idea, and after teary nights of promises, he convinced his wife—she of stately homes and multiple cooks—to make lunch to sell to those sugar men who waited, squatting on their heels in the dark, for the bus to Belle Glade every morning. They worked side by side, Máximo and Rosa. And at the end of every day, their hands stained orange from the lard and the cheap meat, their knuckles red and tender where the hot water and the knife blade had worked their business, Máximo and Rosa would sit down to whatever remained of the day's cooking and they would chew slowly, the day unraveling, their hunger ebbing away with the light.

They worked together for years like that, and when the Cubans began disappearing from the bus line, Máximo and Rosa moved their lunch packets indoors and opened their little restaurant right on Eighth Street. There, a generation of former professors served black beans and rice to the nostalgic. When Raúl showed up in Miami one summer looking for work, Máximo added one more waiter's spot for his old acquaintance from L Street. Each night, after the customers had gone, Máximo and Rosa and Raúl and Havana's old lawyers and bankers and dreamers would sit around the biggest table and eat and talk and sometimes, late in the night after several glasses of wine, someone would start the stories that began with "In Cuba I remember." They were stories of old lovers, beautiful and round-hipped. Of skies that stretched on clear and blue to the Cuban hills. Of green landscapes that clung to the red clay of Güines, roots dug in like fingernails in a good-bye. In Cuba, the stories always began, life was good and pure. But something always happened to them in the end, something withering, malignant. Máximo never understood it. The stories that opened in sun, always narrowed into a dark place. And after those nights, his head throbbing, Máximo would turn and turn in his sleep and awake unable to remember his dreams.

Even now, five years after selling the place, Máximo couldn't walk by it in the early morning when it was still clean and empty. He'd tried it once. He'd stood and stared into the restaurant and had become lost and dizzy in his own reflection in the glass, the neat row of chairs, the tombstone lunch board behind them.

~

"Okay. A bunch of rafters are on the beach getting ready to sail off to Miami."

"Where are they?"

"Who cares? Wherever. Cuba's got a thousand miles of coastline. Use your imagination."

"Let the professor tell his thing, for God's sake."

"Thank you." Máximo cleared his throat and shuffled the dominos. "So anyway, a bunch of rafters are gathered there on the sand. And they're all crying and hugging their wives and all the rafts are bobbing on the water and suddenly someone in the group yells, 'Hey! Look who goes there!' And it's Fidel in swimming trunks, carrying a raft on his back."

Carlos interrupted to let out a yelping laugh. "I like that, I like it, sure do."

"You like it, eh?" said Antonio. "Why don't you let the Cuban finish it."

Máximo slid the pieces to himself in twos and continued. "So one of the guys on the sand says to Fidel, 'Compatriota, what are you doing here? What's with the raft?' And Fidel sits on his raft and pushes off the shore and says, 'I'm sick of this place too. I'm going to Miami.' So the other guys look at each other and say, 'Coño, compadre, if you're leaving, then there's no reason for us to go. Here, take my raft too, and get the fuck out of here.'"

Raúl let a shaking laugh rise from his belly and saluted Máximo with a domino piece.

"A good one, my friend."

Carlos laughed long and loud. Antonio laughed too, but he was careful not to laugh too hard and he gave his friend a sharp look over the racket he was causing. He and Carlos were Dominican, not Cuban, and they ate their same foods and played their same games, but Antonio knew they still didn't understand all the layers of hurt in the Cubans' jokes.

~

It had been Raúl's idea to go down to Domino Park that first time. Máximo protested. He had seen the rows of tourists pressed up against the fence, gawking at the colorful old guys playing dominos.

"I'm not going to be the sad spectacle in someone's vacation slide show," he'd said.

But Raúl was already dressed up in a pale blue guayabera, saying how it was a beautiful day and smell the air.

"Let them take pictures," Raúl said. "What the hell. Make us immortal."

"Immortal," Máximo said like a sneer. And then to himself, The gods' punishment.

It was that year after Rosa died and Máximo didn't want to tell how he'd begun to see her at the kitchen table as she'd been at twenty-five. Watched one thick strand of her dark hair stuck to her morning face. He saw her at thirty, bending down to wipe the chocolate off the cheeks of their two small daughters. And his eyes moved from Rosa to his small daughters. He had something he needed to tell them. He saw them grown up, at the funeral, crying together. He watched Rosa rise and do the sign of the cross. He knew he was caught inside a nightmare, but he couldn't stop. He would emerge slowly, creaking out of the shower and there she'd be, Rosa, like before, her breasts round and pink from the hot water, calling back through the years. Some mornings he would awake and smell peanuts roasting and hear the faint call of the manicero pleading for someone to relieve his burden of white paper cones. Or it would be thundering, the long hard thunder of Miami that was so much like the thunder of home that each rumble shattered the morning of his other life. He would awake, caught fast in the damp sheets, and feel himself falling backwards.

He took the number eight bus to Eighth Street and 15th Avenue. At Domino Park, he sat with Raúl and they played alone that first day, Máximo noticing his own speckled hands, the spots of light through the banyan leaves, a round red beetle that crawled slowly across the table, then hopped the next breeze and floated away.

~

Antonio and Carlos were not Cuban, but they knew when to dump their heavy pieces and when to hold back the eights for the final shocking stroke. Waiting for a table, Raúl and Máximo would linger beside them and watch them lay their traps, a succession of threes that broke their opponents, an incredible run of fives. Even the unthinkable: passing when they had the piece to play.

Other twosomes began to refuse to play with the Dominicans, said that tipo Carlos gave them the creeps with his giggling and monosyllables. Besides, any team that won so often must be cheating, went the charge, especially a team one-half imbecile. But really it was that no one plays to lose. You begin to lose again and again and it reminds you of other things in your life, the despair of it all begins to bleed through and that is not what games are for. Who wants to live their whole life alongside the lucky? But Máximo and Raúl liked these blessed Dominicans, appreciated the well-oiled moves of two old pros. And if the two Dominicans, afraid to be alone again, let them win now and then, who would know, who could ever admit to such a thing?

For many months they didn't know much about each other, these four men. Even the smallest boy knew not to talk when the pieces were in play. But soon came Máximo's jokes during the shuffling, something new and bright coming into his eyes like daydreams as he spoke. Carlos' full loud laughter, like that of children. And the four men learned to linger long enough between sets to color an old memory while the white pieces scraped along the table.

One day as they sat at their table closest to the sidewalk, a pretty girl walked by. She swung her long brown hair around and looked in at the men with her green eyes.

"What the hell is she looking at," said Antonio, who al-ways sat with his back to the wall, looking out at the street. But the others saw how he returned the stare too.

Carlos let out a giggle and immediately put a hand to his mouth.

"In Santo Domingo, a man once looked at—" But Carlos didn't get to finish.

"Shut up, you old idiot," said Antonio, putting his hands on the table like he was about to get up and leave.

"Please," Máximo said.

The girl stared another moment, then turned and left. Raúl rose slowly, flattening down his oiled hair with his right hand.

"Ay, mi niña."

"Sit down, hombre," Antonio said. "You're an old fool, just like this one."

"You're the fool," Raúl called back. "A woman like that . . ." He watched the girl cross the street. When she was out of sight, he grabbed the back of the chair behind him and eased his body down, his eyes still on the street. The other three men looked at one another.

"I knew a woman like that once," Raúl said after a long moment.

"That's right, he did," Antonio said, "in his moist boy dreams—what was it? A century ago?"

"No me jodas," Raúl said. "You are a vulgar man. I had a life all three of you would have paid millions for. Women."

Máximo watched him, then lowered his face, shuffled the dominos.

"I had women," Raúl said.

"We all had women," Carlos said, and he looked like he was about to laugh again, but instead just sat there, smiling like he was remembering one of Máximo's jokes.

"There was one I remember. More beautiful than the rising moon," Raúl said.

"Oh Jesus," Antonio said. "You people."

Máximo looked up, watching Raúl.

"Ay, a woman like that," Raúl said and shook his head. "The women of Cuba were radiant, magnificent, wouldn't you say, professor?"

Máximo looked away.

"I don't know," Antonio said. "I think that Americana there looked better than anything you remember."

And that brought a long laugh from Carlos.

Máximo sat all night at the pine table in his new efficiency, thinking about the green-eyed girl and wondering why he was thinking about her. The table and a narrow bed had come with the apartment, which he'd moved into after selling their house in Shenandoah. The table had come with two chairs, sturdy and polished—not in the least institutional—but he had moved the other chair by the bed.

The landlady, a woman in her forties, had helped Máximo haul up three potted palms. Later, he bought a green pot of marigolds he saw in the supermarket and brought its butter leaves back to life under the window's eastern light. Máximo often sat at the table through the night, sometimes reading Martí, sometimes listening to the rain on the tin hull of the air conditioner.

When you are older, he'd read somewhere, you don't need as much sleep. And wasn't that funny because his days felt more like sleep than ever. Dinner kept him occupied for hours, remembering the story of each dish. Sometimes, at the table, he greeted old friends and awakened with a start when they reached out to touch him. When dawn rose and slunk into the room sideways through the blinds, Máximo walked as in a dream across the thin patterns of light on the terrazzo. The chair, why did he keep the other chair? Even the marigolds reminded him. An image returned again and again. Was it the green-eyed girl?

And then he remembered that Rosa wore carnations in her hair and hated her name. And that it saddened him because he liked to roll it off his tongue like a slow train to the country.

"Rosa," he said, taking her hand the night they met at La Concha while an old danzón played.

"Clavel," she said, tossing her head back in a crackling laugh. "Call me Clavel."

She pulled her hand away and laughed again. "Don't you notice the flower in a girl's hair?"

He led her around the dance floor, lined with chaperones, and when they turned he whispered that he wanted to follow her laughter to the moon. She laughed again, the notes round and heavy as summer raindrops, and Máximo felt his fingers go cold where they touched hers. The danzón played and they turned and turned and the faces of the chaperones and the moist warm air—and Máximo with his cold fingers worried that she had laughed at him. He was twenty-four and could not imagine a more sorrowful thing in all the world.

Sometimes, years later, he would catch a premonition of Rosa in the face of his eldest daughter. She would turn toward a window or do something with her eyes. And then she would smile and tilt her head back and her laughter connected him again to that night, made him believe for a moment that life was a string you could gather up in your hands all at once.

He sat at the table and tried to remember the last time he saw Marisa. In California now. An important lawyer. A year? Two? Anabel, gone to New York? Two years? They called more often than most children, Máximo knew. They called often and he was lucky that way.

~

"Fidel decides he needs to get in touch with young people."

"Ay, ay, ay."

"So his handlers arrange for him to go to a school in Havana. He gets all dressed up in his olive uniform, you know, puts conditioner on his beard and brushes it one hundred times, all that."

Raúl breathed out, letting each breath come out like a puff of laughter. "Where do you get these things?"

"No interrupting the artist anymore, okay?" Máximo continued. "So after he's beautiful enough, he goes to the school. He sits in on a few classes, walks around the halls. Finally, it's time for Fidel to leave and he realizes he hasn't talked to anyone. He rushes over to the assembly that is seeing him off with shouts of 'Comandante!' and he pulls a little boy out of a row. 'Tell me,' Fidel says, 'what is your name?' 'Pepito,' the little boy answers. 'Pepito—what a nice name,' Fidel says. 'And tell me, Pepito, what do you think of the revolution?' 'Comandante,' Pepito says, 'the revolution is the reason we are all here.' 'Ah, very good, Pepito. And tell me, what is your favorite subject?' Pepito answers, 'Comandante, my favorite subject is mathematics.' Fidel pats the little boy on the head. 'And tell me, Pepito, what would you like to be when you grow up?' Pepito smiles and says, 'Comandante, I would like to be a tourist.'"

Máximo looked around the table, a shadow of a smile on his thin white lips as he waited for the laughter.

"Ay," Raúl said. "That is so funny it breaks my heart."

~

Máximo grew to like dominos, the way each piece became part of the next. After the last piece was laid down and they were tallying up the score, Máximo liked to look over the table as an artist might. He liked the way the row of black dots snaked around the table with such free-flowing abandon it was almost as if, thrilled to be let out of the box, the pieces choreographed a fresh dance of gratitude every night. He liked the straightforward contrast of black on white. The clean, fresh scrape of the pieces across the table before each new round. The audacity of the double nines. The plain smooth face of the blank, like a newborn unetched by the world to come.

"Professor," Raúl began. "Let's speed up the shuffling a bit, sí?"

"I was thinking," Máximo said.

"Well, that shouldn't take long," Antonio said.

"Who invented dominos, anyway?" Máximo said.

"I'd say it was probably the Chinese," Antonio said.

"No jodas," Raúl said. "Who else could have invented this game of skill and intelligence but a Cuban?"

"Coño," said Antonio without a smile. "Here we go again."

"Ah, bueno," Raúl said with a smile stuck between joking and condescending. "You don't have to believe it if it hurts."

Carlos let out a long laugh.

"You people are unbelievable," said Antonio. But there was something hard and tired behind the way he smiled.

~

It was the first day of December, but summer still hung about in the brightest patches of sunlight. The four men sat under the shade of the banyan tree. It wasn't cold, not even in the shade, but three of the men wore cardigans. If asked, they would say they were expecting a chilly north wind and doesn't anybody listen to the weather forecasts anymore. Only Antonio, his round body enough to keep him warm, clung to the short sleeves of summer.

Kids from the local Catholic high school had volunteered to decorate the park for Christmas and they dashed about with tinsel in their hair, bumping one another and laughing loudly. Lucinda, the woman who issued the dominos and kept back the gambling, asked them to quiet down, pointing at the men. A wind stirred the top branches of the banyan tree and moved on without touching the ground. One leaf fell to the table.

Antonio waited for Máximo to fetch Lucinda's box of plastic pieces. Antonio held his brown paper bag to his chest and looked at the Cubans, his customary sourness replaced for a moment by what in a man like him could pass for levity. Máximo sat down and began to dump the plastic pieces on the table as he always did. But this time, Antonio held out his hand.

"One moment," he said and shook his brown paper bag.

"¿Qué pasa, chico?" Máximo said.

Antonio reached into the paper bag as the men watched. He let the paper fall away. In his hand he held an oblong black leather box.

"Coñooo," Raúl said.

Antonio set the box on the table, like a magician drawing out his trick. He looked around to the men and finally opened the box with a flourish to reveal a neat row of big heavy pieces, gone yellow and smooth like old teeth. They bent in closer to look. Antonio tilted the box gently and the pieces fell out in one long line, their black dots facing up now like tight dark pupils in the sunlight.

"Ivory," Antonio said. "And ebony. It's an antique. You're not allowed to make them anymore."

"Beautiful," Carlos said and clasped his hands.

"My daughter found them for me in New Orleans," Antonio continued, ignoring Carlos.

He looked around the table and lingered on Máximo, who had lowered the box of plastic dominos to the ground.

"She said she's been searching for them for two years. Couldn't wait two more weeks to give them to me," he said.

"Coñooo," Raúl said.

A moment passed.

"Well," Antonio said, "what do you think, Máximo?"

Máximo looked at him. Then he bent across the table to touch one of the pieces. He gave a jerk with his head and listened for the traffic. "Very nice," he said.

"Very nice?" Antonio said. "Very nice?" He laughed in his thin way. "My daughter walked all over New Orleans to find this and the Cuban thinks it's 'very nice'?" He paused, watching Máximo. "Did you know my daughter is coming to visit me for Christmas, Máximo? Maybe you can tell her that her gift was very nice, but not as nice as some you remember, eh?"

Máximo looked up, his eyes settling on Carlos, who looked at Antonio and then looked away.

"Calm down, hombre," Carlos said, opening his arms wide, a nervous giggle beginning in his throat. "What's gotten into you?"

Antonio waved his hand and sat down. A diesel truck rattled down Eighth Street, headed for downtown.

"My daughter is a district attorney in Los Angeles," Máximo said after the noise of the truck died. "December is one of the busiest months."

He felt a heat behind his eyes he had not felt in many years.

"Feel one in your hand," Antonio said. "Feel how heavy that is."

~

When the children were small, Máximo and Rosa used to spend Nochebuena with his cousins in Cárdenas. It was a five-hour drive from Havana in the cars of those days. They would rise early on the twenty-third and arrive by mid-afternoon so Máximo could help the men kill the pig for the feast the following night. Máximo and the other men held the squealing, squirming animal down, its wiry brown coat cutting into their gloveless hands. But God, they were intelligent creatures. No sooner did it spot the knife than the animal bolted out of their arms, screaming like Armageddon. It had become the subtext to the Nochebuena tradition, this chasing of the terrified pig through the yard, dodging orange trees and rotting fruit underneath. The children were never allowed to watch, Rosa made sure. They sat indoors with the women and stirred the black beans. With loud laughter, they shut out the shouts of the men and the hysterical pleadings of the animal as it was dragged back to its slaughter.

~

"Juanito the little dog gets off the boat from Cuba and decides to take a little stroll down Brickell Avenue."

"Let me make sure I understand the joke. Juanito is a dog. Bowwow."

"That's pretty good."

"Yes, Juanito is a dog, goddamn it."

Raúl looked up, startled.

Máximo shuffled the pieces hard and swallowed. He swung his arms across the table in wide, violent arcs. One of the pieces flew off the table.

"Hey, hey, watch it with that, what's wrong with you?"

Máximo stopped. He felt his heart beating. "I'm sorry," he said. He bent over the edge of the table to see where the piece had landed. "Wait a minute." He held the table with one hand and tried to stretch to pick up the piece.

"What are you doing?"

"Just wait a minute." When he couldn't reach, he stood, pulled the piece toward him with his foot, sat back down, and reached for it again, this time grasping it between his fingers and his palm. He put it facedown on the table with the others and shuffled, slowly, his mind barely registering the traffic.

"Where was I—Juanito the little dog, right, bowwow." Máximo took a deep breath. "He's just off the boat from Cuba and is strolling down Brickell Avenue. He's looking up at all the tall and shiny buildings. 'Coñoo,' he says, dazzled by all the mirrors. 'There's nothing like this in Cuba.'"

"Hey, hey, professor. We had tall buildings."

"Jesus Christ!" Máximo said. He pressed his thumb and forefinger into the corners of his eyes. "This is after Castro, then. Let me just get it out for Christ's sake."

He stopped shuffling. Raúl looked away.

"Ready now? Juanito the little dog is looking up at all the tall buildings and he's so happy to finally be in America because all his cousins have been telling him what a great country it is, right? You know, they were sending back photos of their new cars and girlfriends."

"A joke about dogs who drive cars—I've heard it all."

"Hey, they're Cuban super-dogs."

"All right, they're sending back photos of their new owners or the biggest bones any dog has ever seen. Anything you like. Use your imaginations." Máximo stopped shuffling. "Where was I?"

"You were at the part where Juanito buys a Rolls-Royce."

The men laughed.

"Okay, Antonio, why don't you three fools continue the joke." Máximo got up from the table. "You've made me forget the rest of it."

"Aw, come on, chico, sit down, don't be so sensitive."

"Come on, professor, you were at the part where Juanito is so glad to be in America."

"Forget it. I can't remember the rest now."

Máximo rubbed his temple, grabbed the back of the chair, and sat down slowly, facing the street. "Just leave me alone, I can't remember it." He pulled at the pieces two by two. "I'm sorry. Look, let's just play."

The men set up their double rows of dominos, like miniature barricades before them.

"These pieces are a work of art," Antonio said and laid down a double eight.

The banyan tree was strung with white lights that were lit all day. Colored lights twined around the metal poles of the fence, which was topped with a long loping piece of gold tinsel garland.

The Christmas tourists began arriving just before lunch as Máximo and Raúl stepped off the number eight. Carlos and Antonio were already at the table, watched by two groups of families. Mom and Dad with kids. They were big; even the kids were big and pink. The mother whispered to the kids and they smiled and waved. Raúl waved back at the mother.

"Nice legs, yes," he whispered to Máximo.

Before Máximo looked away, he saw the mother take out a little black pocket camera. He saw the flash out of the corner of his eye. He sat down and looked around the table; the other men stared at their pieces.

The game started badly. It happened sometimes—the distribution of the pieces went all wrong and out of desperation one of the men made mistakes and soon it was all they could do not to knock all the pieces over and start fresh. Raúl set down a double three and signaled to Máximo it was all he had. Carlos passed. Máximo surveyed his last five pieces. His thoughts scattered to the family outside. He looked to find the tallest boy with his face pressed between the iron slats, staring at him.

"You pass?" Antonio said.

Máximo looked at him, then at the table. He put down a three and a five. He looked again; the boy was gone. The family had moved on.

The tour groups arrived later that afternoon. First the white buses with the happy blue letters WELCOME TO LITTLE HAVANA. Next, the fat women in white shorts, their knees lost in an abstraction of flesh. Máximo tried to concentrate on the game. The worst part was how the other men acted out for them. Dominos are supposed to be a quiet game. And now there they were shouting at each other and gesturing. A few of the men had even brought cigars, and they dangled now, unlit, from their mouths.

"You see, Raúl," Máximo said. "You see how we're a spectacle?" He felt like an animal and wanted to growl and cast about behind the metal fence.

Raúl shrugged. "Doesn't bother me."

"A goddamn spectacle. A collection of old bones," Máximo said.

The other men looked up at Máximo.

"Hey, speak for yourself, cabrón," Antonio said.

Raúl shrugged again.

Máximo rubbed his knuckles and began to shuffle the pieces. It was hot, and the sun was setting in his eyes, backlighting the car exhaust like a veil before him. He rubbed his temple, feeling the skin move over the bone. He pressed the inside corners of his eyes, then drew his hand back over the pieces.

"Hey, you okay there?" Antonio said.

An open trolley pulled up and parked on the curb. A young man with blond hair, perhaps in his thirties, stood up in the front, holding a microphone. He wore a guayabera. Máximo looked away.

"This here is Domino Park," came the amplified voice in English, then Spanish. "No one under fifty-five allowed, folks. But we can sure watch them play."

Máximo heard shutters click, then convinced himself he couldn't have heard, not from where he was.

"Most of these men are Cuban and they're keeping alive the tradition of their homeland," the amplified voice continued, echoing against the back wall of the park. "You see, in Cuba, it was very common to retire to a game of dominos after a good meal. It was a way to bond and build community. Folks, you here are seeing a slice of the past. A simpler time of good friendships and unhurried days."

Maybe it was the sun. The men later noted that he seemed odd. The tics. Rubbing his bones.

First Máximo muttered to himself. He shuffled automatically. When the feedback on the microphone pierced through Domino Park, he could no longer sit where he was, accept things as they were. It was a moment that had long been missing from his life.

He stood and made a fist at the trolley.

"Mierda!" he shouted. "Mierda! That's the biggest bullshit I've ever heard."

He made a lunge at the fence. Carlos jumped up and restrained him. Raúl led him back to his seat.

The man of the amplified voice cleared his throat. The people on the trolley looked at him and back at Máximo; perhaps they thought this was part of the show.

"Well." The man chuckled. "There you have it, folks."

Lucinda ran over, but the other men waved her off. She began to protest about rules and propriety. The park had a reputation to uphold.

It was Antonio who spoke.

"Leave the man alone," he said.

Máximo looked at him. His head was pounding. Antonio met his gaze briefly, then looked to Lucinda.

"Some men don't like to be stared at is all," he said. "It won't happen again."

She shifted her weight, but remained where she was, watching.

"What are you waiting for?" Antonio said, turning now to Máximo, who had lowered his head into the white backs of the dominos. "Let's play."

That night Máximo was too tired to sit at the pine table. He didn't even prepare dinner. He slept, and in his dreams he was a green and yellow fish swimming in warm waters, gliding through the coral, the only fish in the sea and he was happy. But the light changed and the sea darkened suddenly and he was rising through it, afraid of breaking the surface, afraid of the pinhole sun on the other side, afraid of drowning in the blue vault of sky.

~

"Let me finish the story of Juanito the little dog."

No one said anything.

"Is that okay? I'm okay. I just remembered it. Can I finish it?"

The men nodded, but still did not speak.

"He is just off the boat from Cuba. He is walking down Brickell Avenue. And he is trying to steady himself, see, because he still has his sea legs and all the buildings are so tall they are making him dizzy. He doesn't know what to expect. He's maybe a little afraid. And he's thinking about a pretty little dog he knew once and he's wondering where she is now and he wishes he were back home."

He paused to take a breath. Raúl cleared his throat. The men looked at one another, then at Máximo. But his eyes were on the blur of dominos before him. He felt a stillness around him, a shadow move past the fence, but he didn't look up.

"He's not a depressive kind of dog, though. Don't get me wrong. He's very feisty. And when he sees an elegant white poodle striding toward him, he forgets all his worries and exclaims, 'O Madre de Dios, si cocinas como caminas . . .'"

The men let out a small laugh. Máximo continued.

"'Si cocinas como caminas . . . ,' Juanito says, but the white poodle interrupts and says, 'I beg your pardon? This is America—kindly speak English.' So Juanito pauses for a moment to consider and says in his broken English, 'Mamita, you are one hot doggie, yes? I would like to take you to movies and fancy dinners.'"

"One hot doggie, yes?" Carlos repeated, then laughed. "You're killing me." The other men smiled, warming to the story as before.

"So Juanito says, 'I would like to marry you, my love, and have gorgeous puppies with you and live in a castle.' Well, all this time the white poodle has her snout in the air. She looks at Juanito and says, 'Do you have any idea who you're talking to? I am a refined breed of considerable class and you are nothing but a short, insignificant mutt.' Juanito is stunned for a moment, but he rallies for the final shot. He's a proud dog, you see, and he's afraid of his pain. 'Pardon me, your highness,' Juanito the mangy dog says. 'Here in America, I may be a short, insignificant mutt, but in Cuba I was a German shepherd.'"

Máximo turned so the men would not see his tears. The afternoon traffic crawled eastward. One horn blasted, then another. He remembered holding his daughters days after their birth, thinking how fragile and vulnerable lay his bond to the future. For weeks, he carried them on pillows, like jeweled china. Then the blank spaces in his life lay before him. Now he stood with the gulf at his back, their ribbony youth aflutter in the past. And what had he salvaged from the years? Already, he was forgetting Rosa's face, the precise shade of her eyes.

Carlos cleared his throat and moved his hand as if to touch him, then held back. He cleared his throat again.

"He was a good dog," Carlos said and pressed his lips together.

Antonio began to laugh, then fell silent with the rest. Máximo started shuffling, then stopped. The shadow of the banyan tree worked a kaleidoscope over the dominos. When the wind eased, Máximo tilted his head to listen. He heard something stir behind him, someone leaning heavily on the fence. He could almost feel the breath. His heart quickened.

"Tell them to go away," Máximo said. "Tell them, no pictures."

Hurricane Stories

I know a man who likes the seashore after a storm. Late summer afternoons, after the rain, we sit on the sand and watch the last of the heavy clouds blow out over the ocean. He points out shapes in the clouds and I tell him stories I hope will make him remember me.

One afternoon the thick wind in the dunes reminds me of another time. I see him sitting apart from me, tracing his finger in the sand, and I feel a story welling in me. I begin to tell him about the hurricane of 1972.

I tell him how all that summer the rain had come down hard. My father stared at the sky and said the clouds had turned bad. The days started hot and ended in a tangle of trees. Even the animals knew something was coming. But I was a girl and the summer was long and glorious and the wind that blew before the rain in early morning swayed the boughs of the oak tree. Wedged between two branches, I swayed with it and dreamed the live oak was my house and this was the elegant drawing room and there rested the fine china that we left behind the night we left Havana for good.

I tell him how I ignored the first drops when they began to fall. I lingered after the shadows dulled into dark afternoon. And not until my mother opened the kitchen window to call for me did I climb down and go inside, imagining myself the hero, chased by lightning.

I tell him how I sat by the window through the storms that summer, watching the rain. He says he understands. But he grew up with snow in the winter and fir trees against gray skies. I had Florida. The smell of electricity. Asphalt cooling in wisps of steam. Raindrops that blow sidelong in the wind. Not everyone knows what these things mean. I watch him and think, Was it always this way between us?

Word of a hurricane in the far Atlantic finally came in early August. All those long weeks, the rain had been trying to tell us. It was the only way the summer could have ended.

The hurricane had a name, a woman's name—they were all women then—but I've forgotten it. We saw her first as a white swirl on a newspaper map, a square the size of a playing card in the left-hand corner of the weather page. A small headline said, Storm Threatens Islands. The following day, the map had moved to the front page. The white swirl was painted larger now and this time Miami was marked with a star, not two inches from the storm.

"Were you afraid?" he asks.

I stop and look at him. His eyes are fixed on the clouds, which almost touch the horizon now. The wind blows his hair onto his face.

I think, What do you know of fear?

I say, "I thought it was exciting."

I tell him the storm had seemed so close, explain that when you are twelve the lines on a map seem irrefutable. I say I still believed you could take a running jump off Key West and land in Havana. It sounds true. What am I trying to tell him? Day after day, I burden my flat Florida childhood with meaning as he sits on the sand and waits for night to swallow the pictures in the clouds. We still don't tell each other everything.

I don't know if he would understand that those summer days when the storm was a painted whirl with a woman's name, the sky had been an unbelievable blue. That the wind stopped blowing in the mornings and the rain ceased. Would he believe me if I talked of luminescent days when every green leaf seemed to stop its wild summer thrashing as if to wait with the rest of us?

I consider his question. Then I tell him how those mornings, I laid the paper flat on the kitchen table and traced the storm with my fingers. We hung a map on the refrigerator door and plotted her path. I dreamt of Miami and its little star on the map.

Two days before the storm, the sky clouded. My father folded the lawn chairs and piled them over the lawn mower in the utility room. In the shadow of the black clouds, my father cut back the branches of his orange trees. He scanned the yard for rusted cans, forgotten toys. I heard him whistling as he pushed his foot along the tall grass at the foot of the fence. Our next-door neighbor walked across his yard and gestured toward my father's pruning shears. They talked across the fence. I hadn't seen Mr. Hanson since two summers ago. From the Florida room, I watched my father pointing with his chin, Mr. Hanson with both thumbs hooked into the belt loops of his jeans. Our neighbor laughed and my father patted him on the shoulder. My father handed him the shears, then jumped the fence. For an hour, they walked around his yard, my father pointing, our neighbor cutting. Through the open windows, when he got close enough to the fence, I could hear my father whistling the same song over and over again.

"What was he whistling?"

I still remember. Astor Piazzolla. Verano Porteño.

"Astor Piazzolla," he says. "I saw him once. Did I ever tell you? The summer I spent in Argentina."

I imagine him in an old city, cobblestones and wine, the sky gray and tight, and I wonder how many stories he keeps.

"You spent a summer in Argentina?"

He shrugs and I can see by the way he's bent his eyebrows that he is remembering something or someone. I think he is not like someone I know; he is a dream in reverse.

In the afternoon, my mother asked if I wanted to go with her to Publix. We circled the parking lot three times, looking for a space. Once, my mother leaned long and hard on the horn. When she turned her head to look behind her, I saw her biting her lower lip, as she did when she was worried or was trying not to smile. We parked, finally, at the far end of the shopping mall, in front of a health food store I had never noticed before.

The last time I had seen so many people in the supermarket was on Christmas Eve. All fourteen registers were open and the lines at each stretched into the food aisles. I can still remember the clang of all those registers, people shouting across shopping carts that overflowed with cans.

"The Sterno! Ask if they sell Sterno!"

Children ran around the store, unattended. Women in hair rollers pushed carts. Men in flip-flops flung cans of beans, any beans, into their baskets.

My mother, who never let us have sweets, turned in to the candy lane. She scooped up bars of chocolate, bags of M&M's. But I didn't say anything, afraid I'd wake up and find myself in the vegetable aisle, my mother reaching for another bag of broccoli, our lives going on as before.

"We have to be ready for anything," my mother said. She winked at me like this was a secret, just for us.

He wants to know what else we bought that day. But I've forgotten. "You of all people should remember what you ate," he says.

What does he mean by that? I turn to see him waiting for me. The fading daylight that was like the thin sleep before dreaming now seems muddy and sad. I watch him fold his hands and then he says he's sorry, to go on, it's okay.

The day before began with the kind of rain we usually got in winter. Skinny drops that fell close together. By lunchtime, the wind began to blow the rain. My father said he couldn't wait any longer.

I helped him carry the lengths of plywood from the shed to the front of the house, holding the sheets over my head. My mother ran outside twice to say I was going to catch cold and couldn't my father call Mr. Hanson to help. But I jumped up and down inside a puddle to show her I wasn't afraid. My mother looked at the sky and then back at us.

"Marta said the television is predicting tomorrow night," she said and closed the door. Two minutes later, she was back outside, wearing a black plastic raincoat.

"I couldn't stay inside and watch you two working out here," she said.

"Well, then, welcome to Castle Fortification Project Number One," my father said, and my mother and I giggled.

Each window took half an hour. My father stood atop a ladder.

"Plywood," he'd say. And my mother would hand him a sheet.

"Lug nuts." And I'd pass him one of the silver screws from my pocket.

We had finished the front of the house when the rain stopped. The wind changed direction.

"Funny weather, isn't it?" my father said. "Hurricanes are like that."

He climbed off the ladder and turned to my mother.

"Do you remember the storm of '37?"

"I don't think so. We lived inland then."

"Still, you'd have to remember." He turned to me now. "Our family lived one street in from the beach, across from the park. I was only a few years younger than you are now. It was the end of the summer.

"That's when the worst of them come, after the summer has heated the earth," he said. "They didn't have radar back then, so people had to be smarter, notice the smallest things. My mother had watched the birds roosting earlier and earlier every day. The wind was funny, as it is now. And the day before we had received a telegram from the Dominican Republic, warning of high seas."

My father moved the ladder to another window and climbed up. "Plywood. Thank you. All the cousins came to stay with us. They lived together in a white house on the beach. Lug nuts. Our house was big enough for everyone, but it probably wasn't much safer."

"Why'd they come then?" I asked.

"Well, I don't know," my father said. "I suppose no one wanted to be alone when the storm hit. It was all fun for us kids, of course. My father let us eat dinner that night on the floor of the living room. The table wasn't big enough for everyone. Even Girasol, the cook, ate with us, crouched beside my father's armchair."

"Did the house stand?" my mother asked.

"Oh yes. But little else did. You know what you remember most about hurricanes?"

My father stepped off the ladder and joined us on the ground, wiping his hands on his jeans. "The noise, that's what you remember. Really, you think about the wind and rain, but what stays with you is the noise. Louder and louder and the whole world seems like it's going to split down the middle."

"Your poor parents," my mother said.

My father nodded. "They say the seas joined over Varadero. That's how bad it was. In the morning, all you noticed was the sky. So much of it suddenly. Palm trees knocked to the floor. Coconuts like pebbles in the street. The sand had piled so high in front of the door that we couldn't open it. We had to crawl through the kitchen window to get outside."

It had started to rain again.

"They are terrible things, hurricanes," my father said. "Nothing to play around with."

We were quiet. My father began to whistle. The rain splashed steadily around us, marking soft dark ovals on the plywood. The sky had grown dark and seemed to have shifted closer to the ground. The wind swirled fallen leaves in circles around my feet.

"Do you think he was telling the truth?" he asks.

"The truth?"

"About the seas joining. I don't see how that could happen."

I stop to think. "I never thought about it," I say. "It seemed real the way he told it. Why couldn't it be?"

"I just don't think it's possible."

I remember something else my father used to say: It could be true and never have happened. But he wouldn't understand. This man who is like a straight line, an idea without interruption. I'm afraid if I stop talking, if I say something that makes his eyes narrow, that his love will disappear back into the folds of all those stories he hasn't told me.

I look away. "We only come here after storms," I say.

"What are you saying?"

"Nothing. I'm just noticing."

Every day, I feel him slipping in ever-widening arcs from me. When he returns, when I see in his eyes that things are like before, I know that the next time he will go farther, take longer to come back. I keep talking and think I could talk forever.

I woke that morning, a Monday, to my parents' whispering in the room next to mine. I couldn't tell the time. Because of the plywood on the windows, the house was in perpetual deep night. The hall light lit up the crack under my door like a fluorescent tube. I had dreamt of a house full of cousins. Seen big sky. Coconuts raining down. Waves that climbed higher and higher, joining the seas over Florida, leaving everything flat and beautiful and clean.

The branches of a laurel rubbed against the plywood at my window. The wind raced its own whistle through the space between the wood and the glass. I was thinking of the hurricane stories I would tell my friends at school in September. You wouldn't believe the noise. Like the world splitting open. But then, they'd have stories of their own. It would be all we talked about.

My mother opened my door, flooding the room with light.

"Your father's making omelets."

I skipped out of bed and into the bright hallway.

Usually, we ate breakfast quietly, respecting everyone's waking-up time and watching as the sun slowly lit up the kitchen. But that day the kitchen light glowed against the plywood-darkened windows. And the weatherman's voice came to us from the next room as we ate, making it sound as if the house were full of people.

My father called work after breakfast to say he wouldn't be going in and that everyone else should go home after lunch.

"Oh no, now what am I going to do all day?" my father teased.

"We'll pop some popcorn," I said, jumping up and down.

"Now? But we just ate breakfast!"

My father looked at my mother, who shrugged.

"Let's pop some popcorn!" he said.

The sun has almost gone down and the wind off the ocean is cool now. He holds my hand on the sand.

"Strange," he says.

"What?"

"Popcorn. Like a movie."

"Well, what would you have done?" And I don't know why I'm angry about it.

He leans back and looks at me. I wait a whole minute before I speak again. I want to make him afraid the way I am afraid.

We sat all morning in front of the television eating popcorn and listening to the weatherman talk about barometric pressure and ocean currents. His voice was smooth and calm and his arms moved over the white swirl on the map and over Miami in long fluid circles. We didn't understand everything he meant to say, but that voice was like a dream. And the house was a little cave, shut out from the street. I thought the world could come apart outside and it wouldn't matter.

I ask him now if he's ever felt like that.

"Like what?" he says.

"Safe, even if you're not."

He says he's never thought of it.

We were standing in the kitchen, watching my mother make tuna sandwiches.

"Tomorrow we'll have to get up early and check the gas mains," my father said. He turned to me. "Maybe you can help me clean up outside. There will be branches and trash all over."

"I hope we have electricity," my mother said.

"We might not," my father said.

"The TV said to fill the bathtub with water," I said.

"Good idea," my father said. "Why don't you be in charge of that."

I smiled.

My father began to sing in his clear voice.

Yo soy un hombre sincero, de donde crece la palma . . .

He stopped singing and said suddenly, "The roads might be flooded. We might have to inflate your raft." He winked at me. "You know, it will keep raining for a couple of days," he said. "The thunderstorms come after. Sometimes tornadoes."

"What if the roof leaks?" my mother said.

"We'll have to check it first thing," he said. "Then we'll just take some chewing gum . . ."

He looked at my mother, who couldn't resist a small smile.

My father turned off the television and as we ate our sandwiches, we talked more about what we would do to prepare. We'd put flashlights in both rooms, for when the power went out. My mother said she would put the milk in the freezer so it would stay fresh and cold no matter what.

We sat and talked and then we were silent, having planned for everything. My mother read a magazine. My father turned a page in his book. I noticed the house was very quiet. Not just inside, but outside. There wasn't the usual sound of cars. And the space between the plywood and the glass was silent. I could no longer hear the branches.

"The storm should be getting close," my father said. We sat and waited. The day was almost over when I put down the book I was reading.

"Tell me again the story of the hurricane," I said. "Tell me about the flying coconuts."

My father looked up and smiled.

"Let's go check the plywood again and I'll tell you how we got the water out of my father's Ford."

My father looked at my mother.

"You two go," she said.

I stepped outside and was momentarily blinded by the brightness. I blinked and waited for my father to join me. A few thin white clouds floated west in a deepening blue sky. I looked again. A few thin white clouds floated west. The trees swayed back and forth, gently, as if hypnotized. The air smelled of grass and dirt and fresh cuttings. I looked up and down the street and saw that ours was the only house boarded up. Mr. Hanson's house had tape on the windows. And the Cardellis had lowered their awnings. But my father was the only one who had gone through all the trouble with the plywood. I couldn't bear to turn back and look at it now.

My father looked up at the sky, but didn't say anything for a while. We both stood there outside the front door, looking out.

"Well," my father said. "This is how they are sometimes. They seem to come out of nowhere."

I looked up at him. I noticed for the first time the lines around his eyes, how his left one seemed to droop into a crevice. Above my father, the branches of the live oak played against each other and then were stilled. I looked at my father for a long time like that, his face framed by those branches and the blue sky beyond. At the top of the street, a boy was slowly riding his bicycle in circles. A car horn sounded far away. My father began to whistle.

I am quiet, thinking.

"So?" he says. "What happened?"

"What do you mean?"

"What happened that night?"

"Isn't it obvious?" I say.

"It never hit?"

"Struck farther up the coast," I say. I consider it for a moment and then add, "I lay in bed that night and couldn't sleep."

He is quiet.

"Do you suppose," he says after a moment, "that your father's stories were true?"

I lay in bed that night as a girl, thinking of big sky and coconuts raining down. I saw our house, hugging itself as if it were afraid of what the wind might bring. I heard my parents whispering a long time into the night. And then they were quiet and the wind outside was quiet. I was embarrassed for our house, standing there like that in the dark. I wanted to hug my father, tell him we were so lucky after all.

He leans back on the sand. And I think now, What stories are true? We awake and a lover is gone, has been going and now his body is gone too, and we are left in a clutch of stories. Why do we tell them?

"I used to think my father was a big man," he says. "Do you know what I mean? I thought he would be the first man to never die."

I nod.

"Then one night I saw him standing by the couch with a drink in his hand," he says. "It was the same thing he did every night. But that night I noticed one of his shoes was off and his blue sock had a small hole above the ankle. His skin was showing through the hole. He had that drink in his hand and he was smiling and he didn't know there was a hole in his sock and his skin was showing."

It is dark now and the shore has receded back into the ocean. I think of his story and why he is telling it now. I don't know his father. The moon is surrounded by a white halo, which means rain tomorrow, again.

"Something so small," he says. "And the way you think about a person changes. And you don't get it back."

His voice grows soft, like an apology. It is nothing; the night is the same. But I know that very soon he will return to this shore without me, with only a thick wind in the dunes to remind him. He turns his head, a dark profile against the bright sea, and I want to memorize his silhouette. I wonder what he knows about me. I sit and watch and suddenly there is so much more I want to tell him. About waiting and the rain. About winds that blow storms back over the ocean. That my father was going to be a grand singer and my mother was beautiful. I want to tell him how our first year in Miami, my parents spoke only in gestures, all sound gone out of our lives like air. I want to keep talking through the night. I want to wake up with sand in my hair, all my memories spilling over him like a tide that returns again and again. I remember everything I ever wished for. That summer was thrilling. The wind and the rain. It was thrilling. I want to tell him.

The Perfect Fruit

Her husband planted the banana trees one afternoon while she was away, and for eight years the trees lay quietly in a far corner of the yard, pushing up through the soil pale green leaves that hardened and darkened in the sun.

At first Matilde had been angry. She stood by the kitchen sink and looked out the window at the first soft shoots and cursed Raúl's recklessness. But each day after that she thought less and less about the trees until they passed into a deep part of memory that was almost like forgetting. Now Matilde stood at the sink thinking not about the ancient trees but about her son and the woman he was seeing. It was a Saturday in early March and the wind had begun to stir. It called through the cracks Matilde had left open in the windows to give the wind a voice; and she pretended it was her son's.

She had seen the woman on only two occasions: first when Anselmo brought her to the Nochebuena gathering last Christmas and Matilde's eyes had lingered on the woman's liquid black hair, her narrow hips, the way the bones in her chest welled up like a washboard. Two months later, Matilde and Raúl met them at a Little Havana restaurant. This time the hair spilled over her shoulders and Matilde had to look away before a memory overtook her.

~

After he moved away, Anselmo still visited on his way home from work. He came alone and Matilde was grateful for that. Every Monday, she made a flan for her son, blending in a block of cream cheese to make it smooth and creamy the way he liked it when he was a child. They sat at the kitchen table with little cups of coffee and dripping slices of flan. Please eat, Matilde said the last time. You're hardly eating. And as she watched him push the flan around the plate, she ran bits of his life through her mind: Anselmo skipping back and forth over a lawn sprinkler, Anselmo wobbling on new skates, reaching out suddenly to her.

She saw him as a little boy wearing the red baseball cap that his father had given him years before when she and Anselmo had joined him in Miami. The cap was faded and too small, but Anselmo wore it everywhere. One day he came home bareheaded, his face streaked and puffy with tears, and Matilde's own eyes watered because she knew everything before he said it.

"And he held it over me like this," Anselmo said, wiping his eyes with the back of his pudgy little hands. "And everyone laughed to see me jumping." He had been trying to hold back his sobs, but let them come rapidly now like hiccups.

"Oh my angel!" Matilde cried and brought him to her chest. "It's nothing at all. You're a big boy. We'll get you another hat."

But as he started to quiet down, Matilde's fury grew. She wanted to hurt this other child, this demon boy who'd bothered her son, and the idea frightened her. She took Anselmo and wiped his tears.

"It's okay," she said. "It's okay, it's okay." And the more she repeated it, the more she believed it herself. "It's okay, my angel. Here, Mami will make you some special cupcakes."

When she poured the flour into a blue bowl and it rose like clouds of steam, she thought that was the most beautiful thing in the world.

~

As she watched Anselmo, grown and handsome and trying to hide his flan in pieces along the corner of his plate, Matilde thought of this new black-haired woman. She thinks she knows so much about Anselmo, the way she touches his shoulder and throws her head back for a kiss. Matilde wanted to laugh. It was almost pathetic, really. What could she ever know? The day Anselmo was born, Matilde had thought: There he is and there is not another like him in the world. Now this woman walks into the middle of his life as if she's been there all along. Matilde began to smile, then caught a shadow across Anselmo's face, as if she'd muttered something aloud.

"What's the matter, angel?" she asked. And then, "You used to love my flan."

"I still like your flan, Mami."

She looked at him, noticed the way his cheekbones had come out, the way his sideburns emphasized the shadows on his face.

"You've lost at least fifteen pounds since you moved in with that woman."

"Mami, please. Her name is Meegan."

"You look like a hanger with a suit draped over it."

Matilde felt bad afterward. She wanted to run after him, explain that the comment wasn't meant for him. Wasn't even meant for her. But Matilde didn't know where to begin. Didn't know how to explain that the second part of her life had begun to circle the first.

Anselmo didn't call for four days. When Matilde picked up the phone and finally heard his voice, she thought she could spend the day listening to it like the low wind that called through the house. He mentioned dinner and an announcement and Matilde had said yes, yes, she would arrange everything.

~

Now Matilde stood by the kitchen sink thinking, An announcement? Why in my house? She stared out the window, running menus through her head. Pork? Beef? Matilde stopped. What was out in the yard? She pulled the blinds all the way up, distracted suddenly from her planning. Something yellow out there, amid the orderly, uniform green of the yard.

Matilde leaned closer to the glass. The wind tossed the tops of the lime trees west. Matilde turned her head, trying to see past the motion of green to focus on the yellow. Yes, something yellow growing. At this distance, it was barely the size of a grain of rice. A single yellow grain of rice. Matilde lowered the blinds. She turned off the lights in the kitchen and, feeling suddenly very tired, lay down on the couch in the family room.

~

Matilde was twenty-one and alone when Anselmo tore himself out of her two months before he was supposed to. Upset stomach, she had thought at first, all that food at the shower. Raúl was already in Miami. Her own visa was supposed to have arrived, but there was some other kind of national emergency. Toothpaste had disappeared from the shelves. In the streets, the parking meters still lay shattered where months before the crowd had passed through like one giant, ecstatic animal, devouring the past. Matilde had felt herself physically buoyed along by the momentum, her own thoughts riding the crest of something new and young. Now she walked among the shards of glass, afraid of the crackle under her feet. The streets were empty and silent and Matilde began to cry, gathering her skirt in a ball. She wandered for blocks, the tears flowing freely. The pain grew in her like a fist opening and she began to imagine herself as the last survivor of a cataclysm. She saw herself as from a great distance, a little speck among the ruined glass and metal that stretched for miles, over continents and oceans.

She woke to a white light that made her eyes water. She blinked away the darkness and when she opened her eyes again, she saw a skinny little eel baby, wrinkly skin draped over his bony arms.

~

Raúl and Matilde sat across from one another at the kitchen table, separated by her cookbooks.

"Did he say what it was?"

"An announcement."

Matilde finished her toast and pushed the plate away. She opened *Cocina al Minuto* and turned to the section on pork.

"Yes, but what kind? Did he say?"

"No."

"Did you ask?"

"Are you going to eat your breakfast?" Matilde asked. "I spent an hour preparing that tortilla."

"You should have asked," he said. "What if it's serious?"

"If it were serious, we wouldn't be celebrating with dinner. Don't be dramatic."

Raúl tilted his head to think about this.

"Eat those chorizos, don't just separate them like that," Matilde said. "The eggs don't taste the same without fat."

Matilde took a sip of her café con leche. Then she flipped another page in her cookbook.

"What are you making?" Raúl said through a mouthful.

"I don't know yet." She didn't look up. "Stuffed pork, maybe."

"Well, you know what it is, right?"

"What is?"

"The announcement." Raúl put his fork down. "They're getting married."

Matilde shut the cookbook and got up from the table. She walked to the sink and began washing the pot she had used to boil milk for the coffee. Strips of browned milk floated in the water and Matilde found it revolting.

"Your lunch is in the refrigerator," she said.

Raúl got up from the table and walked to where Matilde stood. He put a hand on her shoulder. He opened his mouth to say something. He patted her shoulder instead, and turned and picked up his lunch.

~

At night, alone in the big house in Havana, Matilde cried for her skinny baby. What if he died without ever meeting his father? She stopped eating. The shelves in the stores were never more than half full now and the women said it had something to do with the yanquis. Matilde started shopping with Anselmo. Maybe someone would see how skinny he was and take pity on her. Near the cathedral, finally, Matilde found an old grocer from Galicia. Matilde called him Señor and tried to mean it.

"Señora," he said and took her hand. It was the first time she had felt a man's touch in more than a year. His hands were swollen and rough and they startled Matilde. She caught her breath and he pulled away.

"Pardon me," he said and winked.

"My husband," she began. "My son, I mean. He is so skinny."

She returned to the store twice a month and the old Gallego always slipped her an extra bit of ham, gave her fourteen eggs for a dozen. The store smelled of rancid lard and old coffee, but its shelves bent under stacks of chorizo, pounds and pounds of flour. Matilde never dared ask how he managed. Instead she let him take her hand and smiled when he brought it to his lips. She felt his gaze on her until she walked out the door and heard it slam behind her.

~

Matilde stood by the sink and pulled on the blinds. Sunlight filled the kitchen. Cloudless sky. But there, in the back, along the fence. More yellow. Ruining the lawn that Matilde had come to count on, that had soothed her.

That yellow, now. Why? Bananas. Definitely bananas, Matilde thought. The single one she had spotted days ago was joined now by a fresh cluster that pulled them all to the ground. Or maybe the yellow grain of rice had merely been the first to ripen. Maybe the others were there all along, blending into the green.

What was she going to do with pounds and pounds of bananas when she had a dinner to plan? Surely, more bananas were waiting their turn. They would ripen, then rot. Then more bananas. Ay, Raúl! Raúl and his impulses. All her old feelings came back to her. How could he, how could he?

~

Anselmo was a year old when Matilde finally arrived with him in Miami. Carrying him, she walked slowly along a carpeted walkway that slanted downward. Where it ended, hundreds of people crowded behind a barricade hung with a banner that said BIENVENIDOS A MIAMI. People carried signs with names on them. Some just stood. Raúl was in the back, next to the doors. But Matilde didn't shout out. When he turned, he looked first to Anselmo.

They walked toward one another and finally Raúl hugged her, patting her back as someone would comfort the sick. Anselmo began to cry.

"Your papi," Matilde said. "Aren't you glad to see your papi?"

All around them, couples embraced. A man picked up a woman and swung her around while she screamed and laughed and pulled her skirt down all at once. When he set her down, she swung her shoulder bag at him and Matilde thought they would never stop laughing.

Raúl took Anselmo from her arms. "Papi's precious, precious," Raúl said and kissed his son. "Papi's so happy to see you."

Matilde watched Raúl. He looked tanned and strong, and Matilde imagined he'd grown several inches in America. He met her gaze, then looked away.

"We have to hurry," he said. "Traffic. You wouldn't believe it." Then he added, "I'm so glad you're here," and he kissed her.

~

Stuffed rolled pork roast. Six garlic cloves, peeled. One teaspoon dry leaf oregano. One tablespoon salt. One bay leaf, crushed. One tablespoon paprika. One and a half cups sour orange juice. One boneless pork loin, about ten pounds. Two carrots, peeled and grated. One-half pound—Matilde closed the book. Pork wouldn't do.

"You don't have much time left," Raúl said when he walked in the kitchen and found her staring at the refrigerator, the closed book in her lap.

Matilde said nothing.

"Matilde?"

"Bananas," she said finally.

"Bananas?"

"In the yard. The trees you planted, remember?"

Raúl looked at her, then turned back to the closed blinds. He looked at her again and walked to the sink. He lifted the blinds.

The lawn that had once been a smooth monochrome of green was now speckled a gaudy yellow. The first cluster Matilde saw had been joined by five others, all pulling the trees forward in a sharp arc toward the ground. Yellow seemed to drip from the waxy leaves like new paint. Already, the first cluster had begun to mottle. Soon it would start to smell.

"What in the—?"

"The trees you planted, remember?"

Raúl walked to the window and put one hand on his collar. He turned back to Matilde. "Bananas?"

Matilde looked at her husband. Thirty-seven years of marriage, she thought. She hadn't noticed him age all at once, that was true. But every few years she would really look at him. There was the year she had noticed his first silver hairs. The year she had suddenly realized he was going bald. Now she stared at him. The way his shirt stretched tight over his round belly, the soft folds of gooseflesh that covered his collar, gave her a sudden and unexpected thrill.

"Why are you looking at me like that?"

"You ruined my beautiful green yard," Matilde said.

~

Raúl had rented a house in West Miami. Two bedrooms, one bath, a porch that embraced three sides.

"This is beautiful," Matilde said, thinking of the curving, fragrant streets of Havana, the home by the park.

"Máximo found me a job in his restaurant," he said. "I'm making almost a dollar an hour. And tips."

"I'm so happy," Matilde said. "I'm so happy to be here."

Matilde spent her mornings walking the length of the street, pushing Anselmo in his stroller. At first the street had frightened Matilde. Monstrously wide. The idea that anyone could jump out from one of the anonymous trees. But soon the trees became old friends with names and stories of their own. As they walked, Matilde pointed out Ofelia the oak and Matacumbre the magnolia and Anselmo clapped and kicked in his stroller with each familiar name. How he needs me, Matilde thought. If I left him here in his stroller he would be completely helpless without me. I am everything.

But sometimes, when they passed the green house next door, the woman who lived there stepped outside and waved. Matilde would wave back.

"¿Cómo le va?"

"Bien, bien, gracias."

Matilde could feel the woman watching her as she walked away. And she'd be wrenched from her dreams again. With each day, her happiness with Anselmo and the trees seemed more like a gauze that wrapped around her heart to keep it from spilling out. One day when Anselmo cried and refused to eat the baby food that came in little jars, Matilde felt finally a great fatigue from which she thought she'd never recover.

She wanted to ask Raúl if he too felt his life tilting, everything sliding away from him. She wanted to ask him if he remembered how she used to read to him from a red book of poems. But Raúl left the house at 7 each morning now and often didn't come home until 9. On Friday and Saturday nights, she didn't hear his key in the lock until after midnight. He slid into bed next to her and let out a sigh. Sometimes he let his hand roam the curve of her hip, but those nights were rare and Matilde recalled their nights in Havana and felt the distance well in her chest.

~

Matilde spent so many hours looking at the yard through the kitchen window that walking through it now, she had the strange sensation of entering a photograph. Up close the banana trees looked almost human. Taller than she imagined from her spot by the kitchen sink.

She brought the cleaver down on the first browning cluster. The tree recoiled. Matilde brought it down again. She was sweating. She'd barely scratched the bough. She held the cluster in her left hand and sawed back and forth, back and forth.

When the cluster finally began to come loose, Matilde yanked and tore out the rest. Immediately the cluster fell from her hand and Matilde almost fell with it, taking her breath in quick hot bursts. She rested a while, then tried to pick up the cluster, but it was too heavy. Matilde decided instead to drag it across the yard and into the garbage can. She was opening the lid to the can when she realized the garbage truck wouldn't come for two days. Damn them all! Why could nothing go right? Matilde hoisted the bananas into the can, her arms trembling. She brought the lid down on them with a crash.

Back in the kitchen, Matilde couldn't stop thinking about the bananas. What had she solved, really? More bananas were growing. And the ones in the can would rot and the entire yard would smell like a plantation when that woman came with Anselmo. She stood at the sink and opened the blinds. More bananas. More bananas than before. Was that possible? Matilde eased the blinds down and walked back out to the garbage can.

She dragged the cluster through the front door and into the kitchen. She propped the bananas next to the potato bin and opened her cookbook.

~

Matilde had been in Miami for three months when the phone rang one night at 10. Raúl was still at the restaurant. Anselmo lay sleeping in his crib. "Oigo," Matilde said into the receiver.

There was a moment of silence, but Matilde did not repeat herself. Then a click, and the tinny sound of an abandoned line.

Matilde stayed in bed the next day, getting up but once to feed Anselmo when she could no longer bear his screaming. Her waking dreams mingled with her sleeping dreams and Matilde floated between all the worlds she had known. She would turn and wake in Havana and even the bougainvillea was where she had left it.

She lay in bed and watched darkness overtake the details in the room until all she could make out was the outline of the blinds against the streetlights. She heard Raúl walk in. She turned to the far side of the bed and prepared to listen to his breathing all night.

In the morning, Matilde turned and saw that Raúl was already gone. She got up and rushed to Anselmo's crib. She hugged him until she felt him relax in her arms. Cradling her son to her breast, Matilde knew she must make Raúl's secrets her own, snatch them from him before they flowered into repentance. They would always be something she had.

~

Matilde peeled the first banana. She squeezed a few drops of lemon juice onto its bare flesh and dumped it in the pot. Then she peeled the next. She peeled fifty-six bananas in the first cluster and then started on the second. She looked around the kitchen. The banana clusters lined the far wall and went out into the living room. Outside, more bananas. She had a dinner to plan. But she couldn't stop thinking about the bananas. They were everywhere. Disordered, growing. All these years she'd patted her life back into place. Now she felt that familiar falling away, the old panic of not understanding. She wanted her peace back, her dishes lined up end to end, the yard green and fresh.

She crushed the first bunch right in the pot with a soup spoon. She poured in a gallon of cream. A pound of sugar. She lit the gas and watched the pot bubble. She mixed a box of cornstarch into a paste with some water. She poured it in. A bag of cinnamon sticks. A jar of nutmeg. She stirred in slow, languid circles and hoped her thoughts would take the same shape.

Matilde didn't hear Raúl come home. She didn't see him stand in the doorway to the kitchen and watch, in silence, before turning away. She brushed away a wet strand of hair and blotted her forehead with the kitchen rag and moved on.

A layer of vanilla wafers, a layer of pudding, a layer of vanilla wafers.

She measured out the flour. She peeled more bananas and mashed them in her own hands before throwing them in the bowl. The milk, the sugar. She didn't bother measuring now. She looked for the wooden spoon and finally settled on the metal spatula.

Matilde worked into the night. When dawn came, one cluster remained, propped against the wall like someone waiting patiently for an office to open. She opened the blinds, letting the rose light stream into the kitchen. She felt energized. More yellow, out there in the green. But less. Less than before at least.

"Are you okay?"

Raúl stepped inside the kitchen. A banana trifle sat on the counter next to four loaves of banana bread, two deep bowls of banana pudding, a plate of banana cookies. He opened the refrigerator. A milk gallon full of banana shake sat flanked by two banana cakes, each covered with thin and perfect rounds of caramelized banana slices.

"Is all of this for the dinner?"

"I don't know yet," Matilde said. "I still have a few things to do."

"They're coming tomorrow night."

"Yes, of course."

Raúl began to say something. "Look, about the trees—"

"I'll see you tonight," Matilde said and handed him his lunch box. Inside, she had packed three baloney sandwiches with cream cheese, two fresh banana muffins, and a thermos of cream of chicken soup. He'll like the muffins best, she thought.

"Eat well," she said.

~

After the phone call and the long night of Raúl's breathing, Matilde had walked through the kitchen as if possessed. She wanted to bite into ripe fruit. She wanted to knead bread. She wanted to beat and whirl and watch dough ooze through her fingers.

She took little Anselmo in her arms and whispered, "Mami's back, Mami's back."

That morning, she boiled red apples and whirled them in the blender. She mashed carrots and blended them with Cream of Wheat. Every day she thought of a new combination: puree of roast beef with orange juice, mashed potatoes blended with peas, peach and mango soups, chicken and cream of rice. Anselmo grew fatter and fatter and every day Matilde forgot a little more. She dreamed instead of mashed guanabana, chirimoyas ripened on the tree, mangoes like summer sunlight, all the flesh gone soft and sweet.

~

Matilde held the coffee can above the burner until the sugar melted into a deep brown. She poured the condensed milk over the bananas in the blender. One by one, she broke in five eggs. With the blades running, she chopped in a block of cream cheese. She poured the mixture into the coffee can and then started another. When she had four, she set them all in the roasting pan with hot water.

Yes, Anselmo used to love her flan. He had that girlfriend in high school who made him miserable and on Saturday nights, Matilde waited up for him with a creamy piece of flan. They sat under the light, Matilde so proud. Anselmo was more handsome than either of his parents. Tall with sandy hair that lightened to blond the summer he was a lifeguard. Oh how the girls called. And Anselmo would laugh and say he was looking for the girl who could make a perfect flan like his mom.

Matilde peeled another three dozen bananas. She made the crust with lard and rolled out enough for six pies. Bananas, evaporated milk, more eggs. She beat three quarts of cream. She dipped her finger in the mix. Then she licked the blender and the beaters and the bowls and spoons. She lowered a soup spoon in the cake batter by the window and sipped it like a fine wine.

For lunch she ate the scraps of lardy dough. She worked through the afternoon. Bananas. Nutmeg. Cinnamon. Cream. Sugar. Bananas. Honey. Matilde worked the loose strands of her hair back into her bun. Sweat soaked her blouse. When she had peeled the last banana and cooled the last pie, after she had turned off the oven and unplugged the drain, Matilde boiled a pot of milk and sat down at the kitchen table to rest. The wind called through the house as before and she whispered back to it, "Sí, Anselmo."

Matilde drank her cup of coffee and milk slowly. Soon the glow outside would begin to fade and she would have to turn on the kitchen lights. But she had time. She sat and slowly sipped. The beaters and the bowls and the blender and the rows and rows of gleaming pots and pans were piled into a tower on the drain rack. The floor was swept. And outside, her lawn spread from the window in a deliciously pure and flowing monochrome of green.

Matilde sat like this for a while until she heard Raúl's car. Then the key in the lock. She sat sipping her third cup of coffee and milk.

The door opened. He walked into the kitchen. Every inch of counter space was occupied. Banana pies and banana cobblers. Banana grunts with globs of cornmeal biscuits. Bananas Foster. Banana flans.

Sticky bars topped with peanut butter. Banana-almond cookies. Chiffon cakes. Jelly rolls oozing thick banana cream.

Where the plates once sat in cabinets behind glass doors, piles of banana brownies rose like miniature bricks. Banana puddings. Muffins in banana syrup. Rum and banana balls. Chocolate-covered bananas. Coffee cake, streusel, bread pudding. Muffins and creams and round little tarts of puff pastry holding quivering centers of yellow.

Raúl stared. And after a moment finally spoke.

"Why?"

Matilde looked up from her mug and motioned with her head out the open window.

Raúl walked to the sink and looked out.

"Well," he said, and when he turned around, Matilde settled on his stomach, round and jiggly like a bowl of pudding. "What's this about?"

Matilde shrugged. "I read once that bananas are the perfect fruit," she said. "They grow anywhere, you know."

Raúl pushed the chair back from the table to sit across from her. "Is this a joke? Have you lost your mind?" he said. "They'll be here any minute. We can't just feed them dessert."

Matilde took a sip of her coffee and milk, looking steadily at Raúl. Raúl stood and walked to the far end of the kitchen. Then he sat down again.

"I had no idea they would grow out of control like that," he said.

Matilde was quiet.

"They'll be here any minute," he said again. "We'll have to order out or something. Matilde?"

All these years, what had she been waiting for? Oh Raúl. She looked at her husband and when he looked away she felt the years peel back.

"There was an old photograph from our wedding," Matilde began. She stopped, unsure of what to say next, unsure if she should say anything at all. "I don't know if you remember it."

Raúl squinted his eyes. "Our wedding! What in God's name?"

"Maybe you don't remember it," she continued. "It's quite possible you never saw it."

She waited to catch his expression. Yes, she would tell it.

"You were standing under a chandelier," she said. "I remember it was a chandelier because the photographer caught one corner of it. Do you remember the old chandeliers at El Nacional? You were standing under one of them, the band in the background. You liked the band. You picked them yourself."

"I did not pick them," Raúl said. "Your father picked them. The singer was a friend of his."

"This is my favorite photograph," Matilde continued, "because in it, for all time, is Adriana Monterrey leaning over you, her black hair spilling across your shoulder like a Spanish shawl."

Raúl frowned and wrapped his arms around his stomach.

"Do you remember Adriana, Raúl? Oh, she was very beautiful. You must remember her. In this photograph, she was kissing you on the cheek. Of course, in friendship. But the camera caught the stars in your eyes. I've never seen you as happy since. That smile!"

Matilde let out a long laugh. "Oh, I fell in love with that smile again, Raúl."

She took a deep breath.

Raúl looked to the window. After a moment he turned.

"Matilde." He put his hands in his pockets and began again, as if he'd changed his mind about something. Finally he sighed. "I haven't thought about her in years. She died, you know. Still in Cuba." He stopped. "Ah, well."

Matilde ran her finger along the edge of her coffee cup. She was grateful for the way he held his hands, like a package, small and round in his lap. But suddenly he stood, shaking himself as she'd seen him do to scare away creeping slumber.

"Really, Matilde. What does it matter now," he said. "I don't know why you should be upset about a photograph when it meant nothing."

He turned to her, a face she had never seen.

"Is that what this is all about?" he said. "Some silly photograph?"

Matilde took a deep breath. Where was the center? What did Adriana matter now? Raúl's women, the late nights, the vacant phone calls? She looked at her husband, so round and soft. She remembered thinking, on their wedding day, that one day she would understand him. Child dreams. We live alone in our own core, flitting over the surface now and then, pretending. Like Meegan, who would never know if Anselmo would be hers alone in his thoughts, in that world that was made up of memories and old desires.

"Everything was going away from me again," Matilde finally said.

The night was coming in through the window and the kitchen had gone gray. Matilde stood. She began a slow walk around the kitchen, her hands clasped behind her back.

"All these years . . ." Raúl said to her back.

Matilde stopped at a pie and dipped her fingers into the cream. Then she brushed away a crumb from a blanket of banana icing. She settled finally on the prettiest banana cream pie, one with perfect meringue roses, petals lightly tipped in brown. She cradled the pie in her hands.

"Isn't this beautiful?" she said.

"What are we going to do with all this stuff? They'll be here any minute."

Matilde lay the pie in front of Raúl and placed a fork down next to it. Then she stood back.

Raúl looked from the pie to Matilde.

"What?" He stopped and cocked his head. Then they both turned. A low car engine sounded in the distance. Matilde felt her heart in her ears. She waited for the play of soft tires on the driveway.

From the side window, the headlights suddenly swung into the kitchen, casting shadows that raced across the counters, over the pies and pots, before finally settling on Raúl.

"It's them!" he said. The lights caught him in the face and he stood with the fork in his hand, not blinking. When the lights clicked off and the kitchen fell away into shadow again, Matilde's heart slowed. She heard the low murmur and then the laughter of the lovers approaching the front door.

Before they could ring the bell, Matilde turned to Raúl.

"Please eat," she said. "I made it just for you."

Why We Left

You sit on the floor sorting nickels and dimes into straight little piles when I walk in. You look up and let one nickel drop. The pile collapses sideways, as if reacting to bad news. You straighten it. I close the door behind me, watch that it doesn't slam. You bend your head and go on sorting, making meaningful metal villages out of your odd change.

It is November in a city neither of us like. The house is never warm and our bodies are wrong for the weather. It is snowing and I still carry a summer memory of hyacinth and rain, Miami dressed for a storm. Here, the cold creeps in unawares until we shiver from the inside. The landlord can do nothing. We stuff socks under the doors. We leave the oven open.

One night, the snow falls hard. It piles on one side of the house like a hand pushing against the foundation. I say the house is listing. You say that is preposterous. I say the move was your idea.

Do you remember how you quoted Yeats on our first date and sent me away with a handshake? I read Yeats all that night and into the next day. I unhooked the phone. I didn't sleep for a week. My brown hair fell out and fine red strands grew in its place. I looked like a sister of yours. My dark skin sank into itself, leaving freckles where it entered the bone. The phone rang as soon as I plugged it in. It was you. I was saying the center cannot hold. You asked me to marry you.

I make lists. Ocean Drive in the morning. The drive west at the end of the day. The color of rain. The breezes that wait for the storm. The green sliver of palm blades cutting open the sky.

I leave them in your drawers. I roll them into your socks. I hear Miami breathing when I shake out the wash.

The less you say, the more I write: elephant grass, manatee swamps, that restaurant on Eighth Street afloat in mirrors like the sea.

When I was younger and looking for sorrows, I used to lie awake, jealous of your old lovers. You told me once you didn't love any of them. And instead of bringing me comfort, the knowledge gripped my throat with winter fingers. So I made up names to love them by. American ones. Brenda. Monica. Christine. Names that could have been mine. Alessandra. Maria. Continental ones like you: Olivia. Portia. I watched you caress Simone by the Seine. The icy breath coming off the water, wrapping you both. You walked crouched against the wind in your thin jackets and tried to disregard the weather. The water flowed black, matching you step for step. The bare trees silhouetted against that dark blue sky. Constellations sinking dizzy behind the solid branches. You walked all night until the world went white along the distant edges and you put your hand flat against the hollow of her back and you bent down and kissed her and were happy.

But all that was before, when sorrow was something I went searching for.

One December night, I come home late, my face wet with melted snow. I tell you I've found a forest where hibiscus bloom from the slender limbs of birches. I say the snow shrinks from them as if they were on fire. I say I found the incandescent grove outside of town, all heat and color. I'd been lost, on an unfamiliar route, and I had stopped to watch the sky, already darkening to that northern shade of blue that is like night slowly remembering itself. I stopped, unable to go on. I could not go on. And there by the side of the road the birches grew, thin needles that threaded the stars, pink hibiscus clinging to them in the cold.

It was not so long ago. We lived in a warm house full of insects. You said we mustn't kill them. And more insects came, our home a sanctuary. They crawled into the night, left their sticky footprints on the walls. They had families in the heat. Our house full of insect children. They rained down on us from the pink chandelier in the bedroom and left us giggling in smaller and smaller voices until dawn came and we found ourselves spent, wrapped in each other's sweat.

By February your piles of change reach the ceiling, metal columns that keep the roof from caving in. You count in your sleep. You put pennies in your breakfast cereal. We walk through the icy house wrapped in our separate blankets. You stop eating and count dimes by firelight. I say I've been living for the last two months in a forest of flaming trees. I tell you how the ground in the forest is covered with wet green leaves and slender twigs as if it were late summer, and the air is fat with the song of cicadas.

In a clearing, apart from the others, grows a tree whose blue leaves cover it to the ground like a shroud. Each time the wind blows, it shivers and drops one leaf to the ground. At night, when all the other trees are quiet and the wind is quiet, the fallen leaves glow blue like the hottest part of a flame.

In January I notice you stop counting. A copper flank of Lincolns is caught mid-march around the tan leather couch. Washingtons stare dumbly from the glass coffee table. You look up when I walk in. I shake the snow out of my hat and ask why you've stopped counting. You hold your arms out and ask me where I've been.

I say I've been walking in the forest where blue leaves glow and hibiscus cling to the limbs of birches. In the forest there is a tree with thick roots that come up through the earth and a thick short trunk. It is the kind of tree that stays close to the ground so that it isn't buffeted by strong winds. But from its base, like stepchildren, grow green branches in every direction, wild with leaves of every color. When they fall, the sun shines through them and they become white as air. It is almost as if they disappear in the light. I tell you they remind me of old letters, lost thoughts. I say each pale leaf must be heavy as a book.

You look at me for a long time. And then you pick a dime from the top of a pile and put it in your pocket. I say don't do that. You say you have to and pull me close. I put my head on your chest and feel it rise and fall. When I look up, silver reflects in your eyes like rain.

I say, Do you remember why we left?

It was May. You had come in late from work, you'd just made partner, wanted to save everything for him. I was sitting alone in the living room, the room dark, the flowers you'd sent collecting light from the street. I looked up, my face in the shadows. You didn't say anything. Did you already know? You knelt beside me. I told you how I used to go looking for sorrow, how I wanted to find reasons to be sad. And now. And now. Even the flowers pulled away from me as if they were ashamed of yesterday's innocence. The light from the street blinked slowly. We sat in the dark. Your hand was warm and alive in mine and when you took it away, I began to scream as if I were alone in a valley, lost, with night coming on. Your fault, I screamed. If you weren't working all the time. If I weren't so lonely.

I watched you walk out and the way your head hung low made me close my eyes with shame. I heard your car start through the open door. I stood and walked and after a moment I found myself outside the room we had painted that winter. I thought I would tear at the walls until my fingers bled. I imagined the walls covered in our blood. Instead I stood outside and talked to him about us. Things you would never really tell a son, about lost nights with your head in my arms, your breath still in my hair; about the way your fingers curled in sleep like a baby's.

I waited for him to respond.

But it was May in that tropical home, walls alive with insects. I sat outside the door and all that came back was their buzzing.

I come in from the snow. My arms ache and my fingers are blue beneath my nails.

I tell you how today I stood in the forest beneath an ancient palm and she told me things she'd never said. How at night, when all the other trees are asleep, she sweats long tears from her leaves. How her old roots are numb where they grip the stone and how she longs to lift them out, lie down in the wet leaves of the forest. I stood next to the palm and felt my feet sink into the earth, afraid to move and rustle the palm's brittle blades. I stood for a long time, listening to her sing an old song of hers. When the afternoon flared just before sunset, she told me of a tree that grows straight and slender, with two branches that lift up from the trunk like two grateful arms.

"She stands taller than the rest," the palm said, "and everyone hates her because her uppermost leaves are green with happiness."

And then she went on singing, long tears falling like notes.

You grab my hands tight. Your hands are warm. You shake me.

Flowers don't bloom in winter. They don't resemble old books. Palms do not sweat long tears. They cannot, even in the deepest sadness, pull themselves out of the earth.

I say, Why did we leave? What was the reason we left? I beg you to come to the forest with me. Just to see. The forest doesn't exist, you say. You let go my hands. There is no such thing.

I say the pain in me was like windows breaking. I say we wrote all our dreams in glass.

You say, We lost a baby. That is why we left. Our baby is gone. You say it as if it were something that you read in a book. As if you could never believe that the leaves that fall in the forest glow blue at night, that hibiscus can grow in the snow, that palm trees remember. You pretend you don't know that our baby lived within me. When I felt him turn, it was like that first touch in the dark, like a single caress you remember for years.

We packed everything, moved west like in the movies. Even after all these months you still believe that leaving is a form of reverence. That your memory could make of the past something sacred.

On the last night of the winter, I stand naked in the forest, under the ancient palm who knows me by name. She watches as the years fly away from me. She does not speak and the forest is quiet. In the morning, she whispers, Listen, the sound of loss. I stand still, wanting to hear above the silence. A bird calls in the distance. The wind sings a song of insects in the leaves. The palm lets a leaf drop like a tear and says, You hear the forgotten lyrics, the undelivered messages?

And then the sound is all around me, like falling in love again, like children singing. I want to lie in the warm shade of the palm and let her song cover me like the ground of the forest. Listen, she says. She bends her green leaves down to caress me and her song is slow and long. It holds everything I thought I had forgotten and I want to cry out, hold her to my chest. I hear the wind like falling leaves, the song of old days. I hear the colors of Miami, more real than when we lived there, the ocean like a giant trumpet swelling.

I want to close my eyes and listen, sleep inside the palm's song.

I want to sing with our son, follow his voice to where he lies. His voice, pale as leaves that fall in sunlight.

Instead, past the melody, it is your voice I hear. Soft and distant first and then sharp, insistent. You are shaking me, shouting in my ear: You mustn't lie down here. It's not safe. Your fingers are cold and stiff. Wake up, you are saying. Wake up.

I want to put my hand in yours. Whisper that the forest is beautiful in winter. Have you seen the hibiscus? Do you believe me now?

You are picking me up in your arms.

Listen, I say. Why did you stop counting coins at night?

You bring your lips close. You can't sleep here, you say.

Lie with me in the forest, I say. Just a little while.

You shake me again. Wipe my lips with your hands. In Miami, we lived in a warm house full of insects, you say.

The song grows confused. Did you see the hibiscus? And then I feel your breath, hot and wet in my lungs.

From far away, the sound of insects buzzing. It is so beautiful that I begin to weep in your voice, your breath leaving me in bursts of song.

Wake up, you say.

Shh, I say, and put a finger to your lips. Don't cry.

Story of a Parrot

Hortencia de la Cruz was an imposing, beautiful woman who, like many women of her generation and temperament, blamed her unlucky circumstances on her husband, a writer whom she thought a failure and a fraud. As a girl she had wanted to be an actress. But her parents—who were members of the Vedado Tennis Club and had to consider how such things were regarded—sent a man to pull her out of the audition line one brilliant Sunday morning and lock her in the house until the silly notion passed. She never forgot that she would have been great but for this indignity and for the rest of her life looked back on it as the tragic heartbreak that true artists must endure. To console herself, she married the first man who told her he loved her. He was neither rich nor educated and for a time they were supported by Hortencia's parents in a Miramar house full of windows. Almost adequate compensation, Hortencia thought, for all the trouble they had caused her.

Hortencia and Felipe never had children, and after the revolution they settled in Miami along with everyone else she knew. By then, the love-glow of revenge had faded and Felipe's malnourished frame and rough manners only incensed Hortencia. Her parents' money evaporated along with the rest of their world and Hortencia and Felipe were forced into a small house in Sweetwater. There they lived in much-reduced circumstances that every day reminded Hortencia of the crooked turns her life had taken.

~

One day, as her sixtieth birthday approached, a bird flew into the house through a door Hortencia had left open. It was a magnificent bird, done up in green and yellow with a beak shiny and black as a sapodilla seed. The bird flew straight to the living room, where it immediately began to amuse itself by flapping its feathers as it hovered inches from the ceiling. Felipe ran in from the kitchen just as Hortencia leapt from her lounger. Standing together in the living room and staring up, Felipe and Hortencia said at the same time, "Cotorra." Miami had lately been overrun by wild parrots, descendants of freed pets. Felipe had read about it in the local paper and shown the article to Hortencia, saying it might make a good story. It sat now in a pile of articles behind the drinking glasses, part of the small fraternity of ideas that Felipe promised he'd get to one day.

"Those things are full of diseases," Hortencia said. She watched as the bird settled itself on the edge of a white lamp shade and began to wobble—with short hopping steps—around the rim of light.

Hortencia stood with her hands on her hips looking from Felipe to the bird. All day she had been resting on her lounger, one arm dangling to the ground, the other occasionally bringing a rum and lime to her mouth. She had not planned on this parrot.

She turned to Felipe, still with her hands on her hips. "Do something before it kills us!"

The bird pranced up and down and finally stood, its back to the window, and began to clean itself, rubbing its black beak through its feathers.

"What do you want me to do?" Felipe asked. "It looks harmless enough."

"Oh Jesus, Felipe," Hortencia said. "Looks don't mean anything in parrots. It's a ball of microbes and wormy ugliness under all that fancy plumage."

Felipe looked up at the bird. "Look at that. I think you offended it."

"What are you talking about?"

The bird stopped and stared at them.

"I think he wants to say something," Felipe said.

"You're an insane man," Hortencia said. "Everyone always said so."

"On the other hand, it is a wild bird," Felipe said and stared up at the parrot.

"Oooh, look at it spreading its germs," Hortencia cried.

The bird stopped preening and tilted its head to one side. It stared at Hortencia with first the left eye and then the right.

"Felipe, make it stop!" Hortencia said, projecting her voice though they were the only ones in the house, the only ones ever in the house. "Please, Felipe."

Felipe looked at Hortencia. Then walked slowly around the room, giving the bird a wide berth. He looked back at Hortencia, who stood in a corner with her hands clasped to her chest. He raised a finger to his lips. He slowly opened the window behind the bird. The glass let out a puff of dust and slid up without resistance. He tapped the screen and it popped out. But when Felipe turned to the bird, it suddenly flapped its great green wings and the house was again a commotion of beaten air and feathers.

Hortencia dropped her hands to her lap with a crack and cried, "Felipe, do something right for once!"

She waved him away and ran after the bird.

"It doesn't understand windows," she cried, shaking a red velvet pillow after the parrot. "Can't you see it came in through the door?"

Hortencia chased the parrot into a corner of the living room. The bird hovered in midair with a great flapping effort as Hortencia panted just below it.

"Go!" she said and pointed toward the open door.

The bird responded with a tremendous flap that sent it higher in the air. Its head almost grazed the roof.

"Go! Now!" She shook the red pillow.

Her round face was pink from the effort and two thin lines of sweat were working their way down her jugular. Felipe crossed his arms over his chest and watched. Hortencia swung the red pillow at the bird. Felipe crouched. The bird bolted out of the corner and disappeared into the kitchen.

Felipe and Hortencia ran after it, bumping each other through the narrow door.

The bird hopped onto the kitchen sink, took a sip from the drip in the faucet, and then with one flap of its wings came to rest on the dish rack, one spiny leg delicately curled around the edge of a white dinner plate.

"It's so big," Hortencia whispered, and the bird shifted position. "I had no idea they were that big."

Felipe let out a little chuckle.

"Felipe, grow up and get this bird out of here!" Hortencia was waving her hands up and down now as if she had touched something hot.

Felipe slipped off his shoes and crept toward the bird in his sock feet. Suddenly, he lunged, but the parrot hopped up to the top of the china cabinet and out of reach. The plate on the dish rack vibrated slightly. With its strange hopping motion, the bird began to pace the rim of the cabinet.

"Oh," Hortencia said and moaned.

Felipe stood staring at the china cabinet, as if it reminded him of all he had yet to do. "Just leave it there—it will get bored soon and fly away on its own," he said.

Suddenly, Hortencia began to jump up and down in front of the china cabinet, her falls resonating through the floor.

"Shoo! Shoo!"

The bird stared impassively.

"Shoo!" Hortencia shouted, still jumping, each fall bouncing the glasses in the china cabinet.

"Please," Hortencia said, clasping again her hands to her chest. "Please, I beg you." She bent one knee in front of the bird. "Leave this house!"

She waved her arms in an arc. Then she brought one hand to her forehead and collapsed onto the linoleum floor.

Felipe stood staring from Hortencia to the bird.

The three of them remained motionless for several moments, frozen into their essential shapes. Man, woman, bird: a modern allegory in feather and flesh. Then Hortencia began to cry, short little sobs that cracked the edge of silence, and the picture came to life again. Felipe walked to her and held out his hand. Hortencia hoisted her own self up. At this, the big parrot sent up such a riot of flapping that Felipe took a leap back. The bird shook itself in midair, loosening one long green feather that floated gently to Hortencia's feet.

"CAWK!" it screamed and flew out the back door.

For three nights after the parrot's visit, Hortencia lay awake in bed, unable to shut her eyes. She could feel her heart pumping in her temples. It was as if she'd woken up from a long sleep and found her real life brighter and rounder than her imaginings. In the mornings, she rose and it seemed even the light coming through the eastern window wanted to speak to her. She noticed things she had forgotten: the texture of dried bark, the scent of gardenias through the open door. She felt she was on the verge of some kind of greatness.

But on the fourth night, Hortencia finally slept and dreamed. She awoke with an unsettled feeling, as if she'd been through a nightmare so terrible that memory, too, had rejected it. She was in the middle of her life, in the middle of Miami, and halfway through a story whose ending she could almost touch. From the bed, Hortencia could hear the click-clack clatter of Felipe's typewriter on the wood table in the kitchen and knew he was already in from the night shift. She threw off the covers and ran to the kitchen in her underwear. This reminded her of how her thighs had gone soft and dimpled with the years, and the way they jiggled as she ran made her angry. Felipe looked up, raised his eyebrows ever so slightly, and went back to his keyboard.

Hortencia let out a loud sigh.

"Forty years at that goddamn keyboard," she began. She moved in close until she could smell the old grease Máximo used for his plantains. "You and Fidel should have a contest for the longest-running pointless endeavor in world history."

Felipe gave the smallest of smiles.

"Why did you chase the parrot away!" Hortencia snapped. "Why?"

Felipe looked up at his wife. Her knuckles were white caps on her fists. Hortencia stood across from him. The red slowly drained from her face like a curtain going down.

"You chased away that beautiful parrot," she said in a whisper. "I'll never forgive you."

For the next month, Hortencia unlatched the back door every morning while she waited for her coffee to brew and then shut it slowly every night after the dinner dishes were done. One night, she walked outside onto the steep little porch that led to the backyard and watched the sky darken, hoping to catch a blur of sudden green and yellow before night blotted the colors. The next, she stayed to watch the stars come out, the details darkening below. She thought, The stars are like a spotlight on the stage when everything else has gone to black. She searched again for the bird. And thinking that its absence sounded like music in the dark, Hortencia opened her mouth and began to sing. It was a song she had not heard in many years and she was surprised when the words came.

Mueren ya las ilusiones del ayer

She sang it tentatively at first, but then her shyness turned to short vowels that were almost happy and the blue-eyed boy from La Concha smiled at her, her in the pink tulle, the stars out and she without a moment to ask who had put this memory here for her to pluck.

Que sacié con lujurioso amor

The young men stormed the barracks as she sang, stumbling over her notes as if they were stones sent down from history. Moncada blazed that first night long, the young men alight in desire for her, all their plans dashing against her stage and Hortencia standing tall, embraced by the stars, night just another name for the black armband of revolution.

"What are you writing?" Hortencia leaned over Felipe to see the words on the paper. Felipe snatched the sheet out and turned off the typewriter.

"What were you singing last night?"

"Last night?"

"I've never heard you sing that before."

Hortencia shrugged. "An old song."

"What's the name?"

"I don't remember."

"It was nice," Felipe said.

"It just came to me," Hortencia said. "It must have been thirty-five years since I've heard it."

Hortencia looked at her husband. She touched his shoulder and he hunched back over his typewriter.

Without looking up, Felipe nodded. "To think all these years it lay knocking about somewhere in your head."

Hortencia let out a sigh.

"You're writing in the wrong age," she said.

Felipe sank back in his chair.

"You're a romantic," she said before turning away. "All that stuff has gone out of style."

Hortencia sat down on her lounger. She tried to let her arm dangle as before, but couldn't find the old comfortable angle.

That night, Hortencia sang the song again, this time slower, altering the carnival rhythm of the original.

> *Y muere también con sus promesas crueles*
> *La inspiración que un día le brinde.*

Between verses she could hear the click-clack of Felipe's typewriter. Before she could think about it, the noise made her smile. She began to pick up her tempo, singing faster and faster as Felipe worked.

> *Con candor el alma entera yo le dí*
> *Pensando nuestro idilio consagrar*
> *Sin pensar que él lo que buscaba en mí*
> *Era el amor de loca juventud.*

The boy stares. Ah Hortencia, que belleza. She twirls in her pink tulle. You I will always remember, she tells him. She sways in the spotlight they've brought out just for her. It floods the wood floor underneath her new pink satin shoes and the straps are on ever so tight. She looks up and the boy is backing out the door, into the night. The trees come alive again. You are outside, Hortencia. It was all a dream.

> *Mueren ya las ilusiones del ayer*

Your boy is going.

Hortencia sings and she sings. And in one window across the way a light comes on and someone leans out. Hortencia stands on the narrow porch, perched high above the steep steps, and thinks the night is like applause in an empty theater, and then she thinks the night is like nothing at all.

"I don't think the parrot is coming back," Hortencia said. She had finished her coffee and opened the back door. It had been two months, already April, and the smell of orange blossoms held her transfixed on the landing.

Felipe typed.

"No, I don't think it's coming back," she said.

Felipe stopped typing.

"Why'd you chase it away if you liked it so much?" he said.

"Me? I wasn't the one," Hortencia said. She paused. Outside, a lawn mower started and she could hear the shouts of the Martínez children. Sometimes, when the wind blew the wrong way, it was as if the children were in her own backyard. Little children, their faces sticky with red Popsicle paint. Shouting and darting through her gardenias. Hortencia closed the door.

"You were the one who said it had diseases," Hortencia said.

"I never said anything like that," Felipe said.

He had gotten thinner with the years as she'd gotten fatter. His eyes had sunk back into his face, leaving two dark circles behind. It was as if he'd poured his own marrow onto the page and it had left him gaunt, only half human. Hortencia sucked in her stomach and stood straighter.

"Oh that beak was so shiny and black, I'll never forget that," she said. "Those blue feathers."

"It did not have blue feathers," Felipe said.

"You're not very observant for a writer," Hortencia said.

Felipe shrugged and continued typing.

"And that beautiful song it had," Hortencia said. "I'll never forget it."

Felipe did not look up from his keyboard. Hortencia watched him. His back rounded over the typewriter. His fingers gentle and soft on the keys. Felipe had long fingers, like a piano player, made longer still by the thin line of his body. He was plain and narrow like the thoughts of early morning when you can imagine your life as a long line of consequences, a simple fact.

Watching Felipe, Hortencia thought of how she stood for audition all those years ago. She had painted her eyebrows thick and black and lowered her voice, saying Darling, just like Marlene Dietrich. She would have whirled onstage in her pink tulle and afterward, in the dark, when everyone had gone home, she would have fallen into the arms of that beautiful boy and caressed his white doll cheeks and whispered Darling.

"Your problem," Hortencia said, still half caught in her dream, "is you can't stand to be surrounded by beautiful things."

Felipe stopped his clicking and the house was suspended in silence for a few seconds. Hortencia could hear her own breath in her lungs. Felipe resumed the simple beat of his typing.

"Why do you ignore me?" Hortencia said. She walked up to Felipe, standing over him, watching his fingers move on the keyboard, slowly, as if he were only composing music that someone else would play much later and better than he.

She felt suddenly as if she'd woken and found herself in a new place. She wondered if Felipe knew how lonely he had made her all these years.

"Why don't you answer me?" she asked quietly, asking not to be heard.

She waited.

"I'll tell you why," she said. "I know why. You've poured all your passions into that stupid story."

Felipe continued typing, but looked up at her, his eyes soft. He looked down again and let several minutes pass.

"At least I'm doing something," Felipe said finally, his voice a bare whisper above the typing of the keys, which continued their steady clapping, as if they lived independently of him now.

Hortencia turned away. Not even she knew her thoughts.

"And the parrot," she said after a while.

"It's not coming back," he said.

She waited a long time before answering.

"No," she said. "It's not."

Her heart pounds as she stands on the narrow porch. The leaves move in a light breeze. And the rustling and the faint call of the keyboard swell like a great orchestra and Hortencia reaches for her song, the notes now afloat, light and impossible to hold. They run away from her, though she tries to think only of Moncada, of the young men fighting through the music.

Y muere también con sus promesas crueles.

Oh Hortencia, the quiver in your voice makes me weep. The boy in the front row wants to love you. The tables are gathered in circles and the candlelight is like a flood where you will drown. There's something I want to tell you, Hortencia. Step closer. See how the night shines.

You could have joined the church choir, Hortencia. When you got to Miami, Mirta asked you to join and you said no. And what of the theater on Eighth Street? The young kids full of dreams they still wore like golden armbands? The lights outside bulbous and red like a bordello's.

You were waiting for bigger things. You deserved bigger things.

Sing, Hortencia. The lights are out all over Miami. The boy in the front row adores you, see how he stares. You are beautiful and you are soaring out of reach, over the night on your own voice and all the men weep for you.

Felipe imagines how she begins to run before she leaps, flying into her night stage. In his mind, on the tattered canvas of the past he still carries, he paints a bird with great wings moving to embrace him. He hears the beating of blue feathers in his chest and turns from the window a nd the moon shadow that is already gliding away from him.

The typewriter is music. His long fingers find the keys like a lover in the dark.

Hortencia de la Cruz was an imposing, beautiful woman.

Confusing the Saints

Long ago, before this story began, the orishas took a look at the warm new world forming at their feet, the green hills and the sky filling with blue, and decided it should be theirs alone. The thin new trees, the boiling new sea—why share it with the All-Powerful, who was too far away to enjoy it anyway? And so they entered into a quarrel with Him. Night meetings, cells, plots, the diagram of a coup written on a grain of sand.

And that grain of sand flew to heaven. Or an informant sold the plans for a single blade of grass. And the All-Powerful shook the back of the clouds with his anger and cursed the orishas. He ordered the rain to stop. He held back the water. In Miami, the palm trees shriveled and the ocean receded to Havana.

Felipe at the restaurant says to make an offering to Santa Barbara. He says Santa Barbara protects travelers and sailors. But I think Felipe has it wrong. It's someone else who protects men lost in dark waters. Santa Barbara you only think about when it thunders. And who's thinking about thunder when it hasn't rained for weeks and every day we get a new group of rafters, red and dry from the sun, and not one of them is Orlandito.

By the calendar, it's been almost a week since I talked to his parents. It was well after midnight and I was dreaming of tiny fingers that held me fast to the sheets, a distant bell that warned me of never waking again. When the phone finally tore me from sleep, I picked it up with sweating hands. I heard the crackle of a terrible connection and knew. And then there I was, screaming into the phone the way we all end up talking to Cuba. His mother cried so much that I couldn't understand and I screamed louder for her to calm down. Then there was a crash and I thought I had lost the call and I began to scream, OYE OYE. That's when his father came on. He was trying to be calm even though he was yelling too. Listen, he said, and there was more static. And then I heard him say Orlandito. And I screamed QUE PASA. "Orlandito," he said raising his voice again, "left this morning."

I dropped the phone. Dropped it with a clack on the floor and I could still hear his father's faraway voice calling Clarita, Clarita. And all that static cutting in like metal in his throat.

I begged him not to do it. Begged him. I sent him more than a dozen letters. I don't even know if he can swim. And this makes me want to pull down the sky. I don't even know if my own husband can swim.

The next morning, I called Máximo at the restaurant and said I couldn't go in and when he started asking questions, I hung up. When the phone rang again, I didn't answer. Then I worried that it had been Orlandito and I called the restaurant and asked for Máximo. "Did you just try to call?" "Yes," he said, and I hung up again. I lay in bed and looked out the window at the wide blue of the sky. A flock of white birds flew by around noon and then they were gone and the sky was blue and hot again. I put the phone next to my pillow and waited. I thought of calling my mother, but I worried that I would miss his call. So I lay very still, my fingers dead, my arms dead, a weakness so complete that I imagined my breath turning to stone. I thought of Orlandito breathing, his lungs alive beneath his chest. And I was filled then with a certainty that he lived. That it was his voice I heard inside my thoughts. I got up and walked around the room. I felt the blood back in my fingers. I leaned out the window. The sky was bare and dry, its blue happiness drowning every memory of rain. Below, a paper cup floated on a small wind. I followed it with my eyes as it slid along the gutter and lifted into the street. It turned in circles and then rolled beneath a car, falling under its own shadow.

~

When I was a child and something was lost, my grandmother prayed to Santa Gema. Money, jewelry, papers. If she could, Santa Gema returned them. When my mother lost a pair of emerald earrings she had smuggled out of Cuba, the whole family held hands around the lemon tree in the backyard while my grandmother prayed to Santa Gema. Weeks went by. At the beginning of the summer, my father went out to trim the lemon tree and as he climbed up into the branches, he saw something reflecting the sunlight. My mother's earrings sat in a crook, a tiptoe beyond arm's reach. They were as shiny as the day she had reached up and set them there before gardening or as the day Santa Gema plucked them from oblivion and saw fit to return them.

"Santa Gema, blessed Santa Gema," I whisper. But then I am tired and want to dream a long dream of lightning and rain.

I sit at the counter telling Felipe the same story over and over. Felipe bends his long fingers around a rag and listens, quiet, his face long and gray.

Orlandito's parents woke to find his note—"Mami, Papi: Los quiero, pero este lugar no sirve pa' nada." That's it. He didn't sign it, but his parents burned it in the ashtray, afraid of where such papers can travel on their own. I tell Felipe that it doesn't bother me that Orlandito didn't mention me. I know he was tired sore of his country and of course that's what would be on his mind when he got the courage to leave. Still, I think he could have said something about me, about being reunited with his wife.

He doesn't regret marrying me, does he?

Felipe shakes his head and smooths the rag on his lap. He reaches out to touch my hair.

"Don't say those things," he says. "The saints punish that kind of talk."

But one month has gone without rain. Almost two weeks without my husband. And my fears pursue me. I abandon them for sleep and in the morning they return, bald-headed and rested as if night had restored them instead of me. They whisper that maybe Orlandito just wanted to disappear, erase the idea of knowing me. They look me up and down and snicker at one another. Poor thing, they say, he married her just to get out and she can't even see it.

I met him in Havana, in my grandmother's house where photographs of serious people covered the pits in the concrete walls. All night, the old women had been holding their hands to my face, telling me stories about myself that I couldn't remember. I saw him walk in with a small bag that he handed to my grandmother. And then I watched him greet the others, each with a hug, the tiny old women disappearing for a moment in his arms. My grandmother walked to where I stood watching and whispered, "The eyes don't age."

I thought, What a hard thing to have to wait until old age to receive a hug from a man like Orlandito. To have to wait until the years have chastened me, deemed me safe. I wondered who he loved. I'd lived as myself long enough to know that men like Orlandito don't love women like me. Sometimes I'll go days without looking in a mirror for longer than it takes to brush my teeth. And then I'll pass a long shiny window and wonder about the plump girl with frizzy brown hair looking back. And then it's impossible not to believe that Orlandito didn't marry me just to get out of Cuba.

He had that easy way that beautiful people have around the rest of us. Trying hard to pretend they don't notice how conversation slows around them. When, after the cake and wine, he finally walked up to me, the first thing he said was that my hands were cold. I thought he would take them in his and warm them. So what if that is what I wished? But he didn't. Instead, Orlandito patted me on the back. He smiled and bowed. He said that he was pleased to meet me and he shook my hand. At the end of the evening, he gave me a kiss on the cheek, no more tender than the one he gave my grandmother. That night I lay in bed listening to the drip of a faucet and willed myself to forget him.

Today, Wednesday, the Coast Guard rescued twenty-three Cuban refugees, two made it to South Beach on their own, attracting a crowd of beachgoers, and one died on the way to the hospital. Fifty-five Haitian refugees were rescued near the Bahamas and returned before evening. On television, the weatherman said it hadn't rained for thirty-five days straight because of a high-pressure system over the Atlantic. It's one of the worst droughts in Miami's history and we've been told to not waste water. The earth has started to crack.

The day after the party, Orlandito returned during the noontime meal. My grandmother rolled her eyes. This boy has perfect timing, she said so only I could hear. Then she turned to him. "Clarita ate the last of the picadillo, so you'll have to content yourself with plain rice today."

Orlandito put his hands in his pockets and shrugged. "Gracias, Señora," he said. "But I've already eaten."

He'd come by, he said, to show me something. First I thought he was playing a game, working out an old joke between them. But my grandmother stood in the kitchen with one plate aloft and looked at him. Finally she gave out a breath halfway between a sigh and a laugh. She walked back to the sink without saying a word. And then I didn't think of why he came. I stood and followed him out the door.

We walked through the narrow streets of Old Havana, all the city in the streets, old men with their skinny dogs, beautiful mulatas in tight red pants, young men in shirtsleeves, their feet bare on the cobblestone. A woman sang a song I didn't recognize and Orlandito stopped, listened, and then sang it back. It was late afternoon, the streets washed in shadow, when we arrived at a narrow door, painted yellow. It was like a happy secret in the middle of that gray block. I saw how different it was, how hopeful, and it made me sad, looking up at him, because I had been dreaming this whole time, pretending we had known each other all along. I was the woman he loved, walking through the streets with him. And now standing at the yellow door, I knew that he was an entire world I knew nothing about.

He pushed the door open. The light fell in dusty ribbons from the top windows, resting like a caress on the figures below. Small wooden birds stood next to gigantic apples. Carved shoes dwarfed tiny houses, rendered to the last blind in the window. I walked over sawdust to the desk where his tools lay. In a corner, a carving sat apart, light and speckled, its skin translucent. I picked it up.

"That one," he said, "is real."

I looked at him and then at the pear in my hands. I held it up and took a bite. It was dry and gritty like sand in my mouth.

A week before I was to leave for Miami, he came by my grandmother's house with a bunch of white gardenias. We walked along the Malecón. He held my face as the old women had done. I tasted the salt on his lips. It was December, a tropical winter, dry and cool. The water was coming fast on the seawall, crashing in white sprays. He whispered something and I bent in closer, straining to hear above the waves.

The rafter crisis—that's what the newspapers call it—is almost a month old. Three hundred Cubans have already arrived. Today I saw a picture of a man wearing a new white T-shirt that said Coca-Cola. He wasn't Orlandito and I couldn't even be happy for his family.

I light a candle and sit in my room. Where are you? Where are you? Damn you, Orlandito. I said I would get you over. I begged you to wait. How hard was that, idiot fool? I hate you! You deserve whatever happens to you now.

Oh Lord Jesus and the blessed saints forgive me.

I'm behind the counter thinking about the gray rag that I'm using to wipe up rings of coffee and thinking someone needs to wash it and how hopeless the whole thing is, how the rag will just get grayer and grayer. And then I hear my name being called. I stop and listen again. A boy's voice saying he wants to speak to Clarita Fuentes. My lungs become small cold marbles in my chest. Messengers in the middle of the day are like vultures. I tell Felipe to tell the boy no such person exists and then I back into the kitchen, not feeling my feet on the linoleum. I push pots into the sink. I grab a sponge and start scouring. Felipe comes into the kitchen and shuts off the water.

"It's okay," he says and takes my elbow. "Come."

The man is about Orlandito's age. Or even younger, so thin and brown. He fidgets in place.

"Señorita Clarita," he says, looking into my eyes. He shakes his head. "Señora, pardon me. I recognized you from the photo he had."

I cannot speak, only nod by closing my eyes from his gaze. I think, Had, had? Just like that, the past tense? I feel someone take my hands.

"I left before Orlandito," he says. "From Cojimar. Orlandito said he was coming a day after me, maybe two."

I open my eyes and he looks away.

"He asked me to find you here. He had a letter for you and a gift."

I look at the boy's empty hands, his thin T-shirt. Had? Had? The boy opens his arms.

"I'm so sorry," he says. "I tried to put it in my shoes, but my shoes. Something happened to them."

The restaurant is hot and moist like an animal breathing close to me. What kind of summer is this, the traffic going on as if nothing, the absurd desert sky?

"Ha muerto," I say suddenly, screaming and backing into the kitchen. "You're using the past tense. You're not looking me in the eye. He's dead! You used my maiden name! He's dead! I know he's dead!"

The boy takes a small step forward. His eyes open large in his thin face. Small drops of sweat hang on his forehead like a fever.

"Oh no, no." He looks to Felipe. "Please, you can't believe that. I wouldn't be the one to come. You must believe me. He just promised me to come and find you and give you the letter and the—the other thing. I'm sorry I lost it. A sculpture. I don't know what happened. We were seven on the raft. I was thirsty."

The boy looks to Felipe.

"Oh my God, what am I thinking," Felipe says. "You poor boy."

He screams back into the kitchen, "Raúl, get me an order of picadillo and some Pepsi for this boy."

Felipe puts his hand on my shoulder and disappears into the kitchen.

The boy turns to me. "He made me promise." He looks to the floor.

"Stop it, stop it!" I shout. "I'm the one who's supposed to cry!"

What kind of thing was happening? Time had a quality I barely recognized, a way of running over itself. The questions balled in my throat. Was he afraid? Why did he come? How many times did he say my name?

"What kind of sculpture?" I finally ask.

The boy shakes his head. His eyes and nose are red and they seem the only living things in his dry face.

"Don't cry, please."

The boy makes a small sound and nods. When Raúl puts the plate of food down before him, he bursts into tears.

Now I know that he was thinking about me when he left. I thought this would make me happy—to know he was thinking about me. But that doesn't matter anymore. I only want him to be here, I want him to be dry and warm. That's all. I tell myself he couldn't have the bad luck to marry an ugly woman and drown in the middle of nowhere, alone under the stars. I say it as a joke to myself, but even then it comes out wrong. Maybe the sculpture was of a pear. Maybe the boy on the raft tried to eat it.

I light a candle and hold out the ring Orlandito carved for me: its surface crisscrossed in a diamond pattern, the inside engraved with an O and a C laced together. I try to pray. But I can't look at this ring without feeling so tired sad I can't move my lips. And I lie in bed looking out at the blue, blue sky, the sun that is drying me from the inside out, and think:

watersharkswatersharksraftssunburnsharksdehydrationwater-
watersunsharksraftswater drowndrowndrown.

Today, Felipe passed me the number of a woman who works
with herbs. I haven't decided whether I should go. I keep
thinking the phone's going to ring. The Coast Guard, saying
"Mrs. Alarcon?" I've imagined it so many times, down to the
timbre of the voice on the other line. "Mrs. Alarcon, we have
good news." And I seize on the Mrs. Because that's what I
am. "Mrs. Alarcon, we have your husband." And I imagine
how I let go of the phone, and the sound of it dropping. I
imagine it so well that when I woke this morning, I thought
it had already happened. And then how terrible to wake when
sleep is the thin blanket you wrap yourself in against your
thoughts.

Felipe asks me every day if I pray. He says to pray to Santa
Barbara of the lost sailors. I correct him, tell him he's confusing the saints again.

He opens his hands. I think of calling him an old fool,
but stop when I see the calluses and scratches like lines in a book.

"Some of those rafts come in empty and others don't," I
say instead. "I wonder what saint can explain that."

Everyone is saying how if it doesn't rain soon, the government
is going to have to seed the clouds. They do that in some kind
of special plane. I wonder why can't they send the plane to look
for my husband?

Oh Orlandito, where are you right this moment, this second that I stare at the cloudless sky?

The herb woman Felipe told me about lives in a house hidden by trees at the end of a street of big, quiet houses in Coral Gables. She opens the door in a red suit, a white handkerchief at her neck, and I tell her she doesn't look like a Santera.

She leads me to a room, empty except for a white rug and a circle of red chairs around a table piled with fresh leaves.

"I'm not a Santera," she says. "But I used to be a saint."

She smiles and motions me to sit. I wonder if I am meant to laugh.

"Your husband is lost," she says, and I don't like the way her voice refuses to rise into a question.

I shake my head to show that she is mistaken. "I'm here to see you about the rain."

"Then your husband has been found?"

I close my eyes. "All I want is for the drought to end."

The woman looks at me and then takes a small bunch of leaves in front of her and begins to weave them together.

"Yes," she says finally. "It hasn't rained for a very long time."

She stops and turns toward the door. A man carries a tray of tea. He is so pale that his eyes are rimmed in red as if he's been weeping since the beginning of the world.

"Please drink," the woman says.

"I don't need anything to calm me," I say.

She shakes her head.

"No," she says. "It will give you strength."

"I don't want potions."

The woman motions to the man. With one hand, he pushes back the pile of leaves from the table and with the other, he sets the tray down. He bows and leaves the room.

She pours a cup for me and one for herself. I wait for her and then hold the cup to my lips, but I don't drink.

"I don't know what I'm doing here," I say. I want to stand, but I cannot move; sitting is much easier. I am so tired.

"You are trying to find the lost rain," she says. "Please stay. I will tell you how."

She takes another sip of her tea and looks up at me. Her eyes are clear and big, like the sea.

"Droughts are very old," she says. "Even though we always think we are the first to suffer."

After a while she says she will tell me a story so that I understand the songs in the grass, the structure of leaves.

She begins in her low voice.

"In the beginning the orishas, the gods of the lesser world, rebelled against Olodumare and plotted to divide his powers among themselves. But nothing can be hidden from Olodumare. He sees even to the liquid center of the world and pulls back the dark cover on the thoughts of man. One night without moon, Olodumare discovered the plot. He took his pain and rage and molded them into revenge and that same night he held his hands out and stopped the rain.

"On the earth, the clouds evaporated before day. The morning arrived dry and blue and at first the orishas celebrated the new light. For seven weeks they danced under the sun. But as they danced, the rivers slowly disappeared back into the earth. The green crops dried to brown. Until the whole world rose in lament, hungry and dry and mournful of all the rain they had forsaken."

The woman puts her cup down and closes her eyes, as if a great fatigue had overtaken her. After a while she begins again.

"The empty sky now seemed sinister, an eye into the wide possibilities of a world they didn't really know. Both the mortal and the immortal felt alone and exposed. They hid in the light of day. And then the orishas began to fight among themselves, each assigning blame to the other."

The woman stops and opens her eyes. She leans back in her chair. Her face is pale above the dark hollows.

"You see," she says. "It has always been the same."

She drinks from her cup and sits for a long while before continuing.

"Only one orisha, the beautiful Oshun who had taken the form of a peacock, rose to offer a solution. She would fly to heaven herself and plead with the All-Mighty for mercy. The others laughed at her, a vain and worthless bird. But Oshun didn't listen. Oshun flew to heaven, the sun burning her feathers, she flew to heaven."

She stops and waits for me to answer.

"Suffering is very old," the herb woman says when I stand to go. "Older than man."

I walk out of the herb woman's house and curse the blue, tell it to explode in flames, go black with smoke, collapse onto the world. I shout to the sky, He's not dead! He's not dead! All you unbelievers will see.

I lie in bed and try to sleep. All suffering is not the same. Mine is the first suffering. Orlandito is the only man like himself, the first with three freckles on his back and long arms and big hands for sculpting.

I pray to Santa Gema to find my lost husband, I pray to Santa Barbara of the lost thunder, and I pray to the Virgin of Charity, reminding her of the fishermen she saved once, reminding her of her duty to Cuba.

And then I pray to the All-Mighty for rain that darkens the sky and brings night and with it the sweet sleep that suspends memory.

We drove to Cojimar on a Tuesday. I remember passing through the countryside as through water, the car heavy, the air heavy, the slow ramble past liquid landscapes. And in me, the weightlessness of happiness. Feeling that this was the reason people continued to live past disappointments and tragedies, for moments when the body floats on its own joy.

Images return to me now in fragments. Orlandito's thick hands on the wheel, his fingers tapping out a tune he carries in his head. His hair tumbling in the wind. Orlandito turning to me, putting out his arm and drawing me closer so that I could inhale the warm scent of him, like the earth after a rain.

The fisherman had been a priest before the revolution and now lived in a wood house he'd built for himself and the woman who had called him into his new life. They were both old and thin, slow to gesture with their hands. They stood in the open door together without speaking, just looking at us. And then the old fisherman clapped Orlandito on the back and said, "Well, congratulations, young man."

He married us on the sand, with the sea to our backs. His wife stood by his side, holding open a book of poetry that the fisherman read through half-closed lips. The wind batted the sand on my bare legs and, behind me, the ocean told story after story.

We spent the night in a room with bare windows open to the black sky. We lay close and listened to the wind in the stars. He warmed my hands in his. After a while I felt him move and then he sat and I asked him what he thought.

"You leave in two days," he said.

I told him we had agreed not to say it.

"But you do and then I'll be alone again."

I told him I would bring him back with me. He was my husband. I was Mrs. Alarcon. He shook his head and turned his face away from me. Not an official ceremony, no papers. Don't worry about the papers, I said. It was a real wedding. I would talk with a lawyer. I would bring him back.

He lay down and looked up at me. His face was dark in the shadow and I could see just his hands in the starlight.

"You are beautiful," he said after a moment. "You don't know this. But you are so beautiful and you will forget about me one day."

I made promises as the night shivered through the open window.

A wet wind has come up. I call in sick and hear Felipe's tired voice like bubbles on the line. I feel nothing. I'm thinking this wind that's come up, the ocean, the ocean and drowning.

I start to think it's going to be fine because these things don't happen to women like me. What was I? A waitress in Little Havana. I cared that I had frizzy hair and what a lifetime of platanitos had done to my figure.

To be that woman again! To worry about those things. Not the ocean that gets into my dreams now, the waves dampening the sheets. How can I say that I still have heard nothing. That I pray every night into a black space that waits to strangle me in the dark.

The sun today, bright in a deep sky. Orlandito, did you see it?

And then, like waking, comes the herb woman with the story of Oshun. Who turned to me and said, "Already you know your husband is dead."

Today, I prayed only for rain, rain that falls in blue drops, that restores the ocean, that blocks the sun. If it would rain, we could breathe again. But there is too much light and a month has gone by without word.

~

I am learning again to fly. The silence is like the open sky I carry on my back. And there is so much I've forgotten. How quiet it is up here and clear. The sun is hot through my feathers, and at first I am afraid that my colors will bleed. Below, a white basin where the ocean used to be, its ribs glistening in the light.

Even if I tire, I will fly. Climb the air like a bridge. The sun that grows bigger will burn my beautiful feathers black. I will arrive in heaven bald and hunchbacked, my face a shriveled countenance for the Lord. And he will take pity on me.

And the rain fell in heavy sheets that touched the earth again with green, a blue restoring rain. It washed out the dust of summer, crowded the sky with clouds. The green hills rose again like the first time, the world warmed at their feet, the thin new trees straightened in the moist wind.

And the rain fell over mountains where yellow flowers grew and over plains of tall grass. It taught the young crops to breathe again and filled the white basin of the sea. The rain restored the blue oceans. And everything was as it should be and the new waters rippled gently away from Cuba as if the island itself were a stone dropped by God above.

Baseball Dreams

1. THE BOY

I have a portrait of my father from before Cuba knew him. He is three years old and wearing pants that come to his knees. It is a black-and-white photo and I pretend that the pants are blue. His jacket has a round collar that drapes his little shoulders like a fallen halo. His hair is slick and thick and he's parted it himself on the right. Behind him, to his left and propped against a coconut tree, is a baseball bat. It's shiny and smooth like a new idea.

His window, like most windows in the house he was born in, faced south to the Sierras. I see him in the summertime; the green mountains become flesh and my father longs to caress them, hold them tight against his cheek. My father loved the mountains. He got up early to catch the first white shreds of morning as they came over the crest. Afternoon burnished the clouds until, black and heavy, they poured over my father's mountains and raced into Biran on long legs of lightning. My father opened his window wide to the rain.

He wasn't baptized and they called him The Jew, and he thought of the black-beaked birds that came to his window to shake off the rain. He imagined himself flying over the battlefields of Troy, the blood running like veins down the hills as he soared above the dead.

He tells lies about those early days. He is ashamed of their ordinary curves now, afraid that the rainy afternoons could have belonged to anyone. He hunted wild doves in the mass of woods that collected at the base of the mountains like runoff. He cursed his teachers. He balled up pieces of paper and marched armies across the rough pine floor of his bedroom. But he wanted, more than anything, to be a baseball player.

To be a baseball player! Like Ty Cobb or the man DiMaggio, who could have been Cuban, a magician from Guanabacoa. My father thought he would make a fine Yankee. Mornings in the hot classroom where the desk splinters got under his skin, my father dreamt of fields of orange sand and white diamonds like life rafts under his footprints.

He practiced by pitching fastballs into the wood stilts of his house. After school, still in the white shirt with buttons, he hurled himself into the clean physics of his dream. Lifting first the left leg, then arching back, hanging in the air, letting loose.

The first time he missed, he stomped his feet in anger and walked away. But the next day, he came back and crawled under the house through the slop, the wild alarm of the chickens. He wiped the shit and feathers from the ball and started again. He missed and missed. But he was destined to be a pitcher and not even an erratic arm would stop him. Each time, the ball rolled under the house, scattering birds. Each time, he went in after it. The slop no longer bothered him. He crawled in on all fours like the animals, inhaling the life stew of the finca, the smell that lifted all of them into polite society.

Sometimes my father would linger beneath the house, listening to the wood crack under his mother's footsteps. Each footfall loosened a puff of white dust that fell lightly onto the animals. Like snow, my father imagined. And then he was in New York, lifting his left leg, about to hurl the first pitch in the World Series. He was Zhukov on the Russian front, men dying all around. Push on! Push on! The landscape gone to black and white, the gray conifers propped against the horizon. He crawled through the ice, to the edge of the hill until the Oriente landscape broke through again, wet and heavy, the tall palms wrapped in blue sky.

The first game took place on the hottest afternoon in the hottest summer anyone in Biran could remember. The boys took off their shirts to the sun. My father had chosen the fastest, biggest boys for his team, but, of course, the pitcher's slot he reserved for himself. He was El Lider, even then.

Without an umpire, the boys had only honor to call the plays. And the first pitch my father threw was decreed a ball. He slumped his shoulders and worked the mound with his toe. He said a fast prayer to San Cristobal and pulled on his pitching arm for a stretch. The next pitch was a ball. And the next. My father caught Manuel glancing at the catcher. It was a quick look, a flutter of the eyes underneath the baseball cap. The boy at bat looked back at his teammates sitting now cross-legged behind home. A few of them laughed and touched the tips of their baseball caps to pull them down over their faces. The sun was high in the sky and the boys cast insignificant miniature shadows in the grass.

My father leaned back, raised his left leg, let it hang, released the ball. He walked his first batter; it still makes me cry.

The boys sitting cross-legged behind the plate suddenly jumped up and began to clap. My father felt heat in the soft tips of his ears. History would record him as a man of many words. But that day, my father kept quiet. He wound up the same for the second batter and when he threw the first ball, he didn't even flinch. He wound up again, without resting, let his foot come down hard on the mound and struck out Bernardo El Bruto. He was no longer hearing the calls of the boys. Or seeing Manuel jump in the air. Only the thump of his leg on the mound, the echo through his hip. Bernardo swinging, slowly swinging, into my father's first victory. It was the late summer of 1935. My father was nine years old. He was already thinking about the man he was going to be. He was already thinking, I like to think, about me.

—Sáquenlo! my father screamed. Get him out of there!

Baseball is not such a big game now, not even here in Miami, a city that considers itself too American to be Cuban and too

Cuban to be American. Baseball here is for the old-timers, the politicians who still see a home run in each defection. The game is too slow, too tame, and too quiet for these times. But I can understand all it meant to my father, a bastard, an immigrant's son. In the straight old lines of the game, he found a dynasty of players to belong to. Baseball gave him rules to master, a history to memorize. On his mound, facing the dark Sierras, my father could be anybody, do anything.

They went three innings without a run that first summer day. Then in the bottom of the fourth, Manuel swung and even before the ball had begun its path against the sky, the sound it made against the bat made my father look away. In his plan, his would have been the first home run of the day. Now he had to come to bat beneath the glory of the boy he himself had named The Horrible. My father wore nothing but his baseball cap and his denim shorts. His legs were already long and strong and burned brown by his afternoons of practice.

—Oye! Brazo de Espuma!

My father squinted in the sun. The boys guarding the bases broke out in laughter. My father swung and missed. He swung and missed. On the third swing, he connected and the ball sailed in a perfect arc through the blue sky and landed, as if providence herself had softly placed it there, in the new leather glove of the only outfielder.

Something happened after that and not even Manuel's swing could save my father's team. By the sixth inning, the sun had moved across the sky, but the air still burned under it. Some of the boys were bloodied by bare-kneed slides. My father's chest was dusted gray with sand that darkened under thin rivulets of sweat. They were behind seven runs when my father took the mound. He looked around. Manuel stood slumped over third base. His catcher sat on the ground. My father believed he would win; that's the kind of man he still is. For the next twenty minutes he became the sum of all the best and worst that was to come. He dazzled the boys with fastballs that seemed to trail in vacuums. Then, just as quickly, the ball left his hand and hurtled toward third base. Or into the line of waiting boys. A curveball that made the boys suck their breath. A renegade pitch that sent them running. Such was my father. And he refused to leave until he'd thrown the inning's last pitch, watched it land squarely in the middle of the catcher's glove, all of it too late, the score gone so woefully lopsided that most of the boys had stopped keeping count.

And then my father just walked away. Like that. Bottom of the sixth, their turn at bat, and my father walking toward the Sierras, the red savanna waving before him like the closing shot in the Westerns he loved. Manuel called after him. Someone ran behind him and pushed his shoulder.

—Cobarde.

—Cabrón.

My father faced the boy, who wore a torn white T-shirt. A cut on his elbow was already filling with blood and dirt. My father heard the shouts of the other boys but couldn't make out what they were saying.

—Cobarde, the boy repeated.

For the second time that day, my father said nothing. He turned to walk. Then spun back and punched the boy in the jaw, quick as a breath. The boy fell onto the long grass. My father kept walking south, the Sierras dark and beautiful where they rose from the savanna.

Judío! Judío! My father walking. Judío! My father walking south, listening to his steps crack the tall grass. Then the fire through his arms, the black-beaked wonder of him soaring, rising, watching the lengths of grass retreat and reappear in bright squares of red and green. The battlefields below, the little men. The sun sinking behind Biran, the Sierras catching fire again.

If only . . . That's how I always start the story. If only baseball had held him like a tender parent. How different it all would be. He would have come to see me on the beach that day. He would have married my mother. I am the little girl who wants a life of baseball rules: nine innings, pads on the catcher, may the best team win.

2. THE GIRL

She was walking with her mother where the water ended and looking down at the way the wet sand oozed up through her toes. The ocean was flat and green like a new lawn and two seagulls dipped and rose above it, casting shadows on the water.

They had come to meet her father, who was a big man now, standing before the crowds, tall and handsome in his black beard, no longer a little boy with a baseball dream. Mirta wore a white dress with three rows of pink lace at the hem and her mother carried her white patent-leather shoes in a straw bag, where the three sandwiches rested.

"He can only stay for a little while," her mother said, and Mirta nodded.

From where they sat, they could see how the beach extended beyond the brush and then began to curve around the peninsula, the green palms fading in the distance to blue-white like the sky. Behind them lay the magnificent wood houses with the curved porches and Mirta saw that one of them, the round white one with even whiter trim, was boarded up, even though the heavy clouds of summer had almost all blown out to sea and the sky was preparing itself for the blue Caribbean autumn that brought high winds and spoonbills and—after Varadero deemed herself lovely enough to receive them—the Americans. The following summer, three more houses would be boarded, their owners gone to wait out the revolution across the straits. And after that, new families would come. And some would open restaurants years later, and new buildings would seem to grow out of the sand. But Mirta would be many years gone by then and the lonely brush that she remembered as it curved around the shore would be gone too and the spoonbills and all that remained would be the blue Caribbean autumn and the high winds.

"You'll never play in the grandes ligas."

"You haven't seen my curveball."

Mirta turned to see two boys tossing a baseball back and forth on the shore. They were the only other people on the beach and Mirta imagined they were her brothers. Her mother, too, sat watching them as if this was what they had come all this way to see.

They sat for several minutes, watching the boys hurl faster and faster balls at each other, their talk growing rough and jagged. Mirta saw her mother look back toward land once and then thrust her chin out. Her silence frightened Mirta, but she didn't know why and the uncertainty frightened her more.

"Mama?"

"Shh."

"Mama?"

Mirta looked at the bag with the sandwiches. She had helped her mother make them, spreading mayonnaise over the sweet yellow bread, instructing her mother, No, the ham first, then the pork, and her mother playing along. Her mother had been laughing and happy and Mirta, wanting to keep it that way, repeated, No, the ham first, then the pork! This time a little louder. No! The ham FIRST! Then the PORK! THE HAM AND THEN THE PORK! Until her mother had said, Basta ya, and put an end to the game.

"The only other man I saw with an arm like that was a maricón."

"Eat that one, hijo de puta."

The boy fell back from the force of the ball. Mirta watched it rolling into the surf and then the boy, flipping up off his back like a fish and splashing after it.

Mirta looked back to her mother to see if she had seen the boy's acrobatics and caught her instead coming up from a quick glance at her watch. She pressed her lips together and ruffled Mirta's hair.

"Are you hungry, cariño?"

"No," Mirta said.

"Are you sure?"

Mirta shook her head so her ponytails lashed her face and sent her giggling.

Her mother lifted the corners of her mouth into a smile, but kept her lips together. Only now, all these years later, Mirta knew how many worlds that one gesture contained.

A yelp once again and Mirta turned to the shore. One boy was much bigger than the other. He wore his jean shorts rolled up at the edges and he had flung off his shirt to reveal a wide chest stained to walnut by the sun. His dark blond hair hung shaggily around his face and matched the bleached hair on his forearms, which pumped furiously in the brightness. The other boy was smaller and darker, but stronger. He wore white canvas shorts and a black shirt with the sleeves ripped out to show his compact little arms. Where the big boy seemed to be taking their escalating game as a merry sport, the small one had grown more serious and sour. Now and then the bigger boy laughed and this seemed only to make the smaller boy angrier.

They had stopped talking now, communicating only by grunts or bursts of derisive laughter, the ball sailing between them like profanities. Now and again the ball splashed in the water and as one boy went racing after it, the other stood on the shore, catching his breath or looking up at the sky which had grown deeper behind the advancing sun.

Mirta's mother stroked her arm so gently that her fingers became indistinguishable from the breeze and Mirta blinked, slower and slower each time, lulled by the sound of the waves and the boys' cries steady and sharp like the call of seagulls until Mirta wasn't sure which was which and the whole world seemed one mass and if she tried, she might be able to make sense of it all in a second. But Mirta's thoughts kept slipping behind the veil of childhood and she whispered, as she drifted to sleep, I must remember to . . .

She was a girl in a white dress asleep on the sand, company for her mother. And now she was lifting outside of herself, she was watching the horizon sink beneath her. On the sand, her two wide wings cast shadows on her old self, the breeze like fingers through the feathers that rose stiff along her neck. She tumbled through the air, the sun warm on her back, the sea distant and soft below, the sound of people like the murmur between grains of sands. And her mother, sad eyes out over the straits, one hand caressing the arm of a little girl who slept beside her and waited.

She woke, suddenly, to confusion. Shouts. A woman screaming. Her mother? Herself? Her heart pounded. She came back to her body in fits, still dreaming she was crashing onto the sand. And then she sat up, forgetting where she was. Fear. The loud voices. Men running around. Her mother gone.

"Mami!"

And then she saw her standing in a crowd at the seashore, the short boy pacing back and forth. Where was the bare-chested boy? Mirta ran to her mother. A man tried to hold her back from the crowd, but she squirmed loose and ran up the other side, coming to her mother's leg first, then seeing the boy face-up in the sand, a trickle of blood flowing out of his left nostril. A woman came running down the beach, one hand pulling up the length of her skirt, another on the short white hair that bristled straight behind her in the breeze. A sun-browned man in white shorts shouted at her and that was picked up by the man standing next to him and then the woman behind them until everyone in the crowd had spotted the woman and some ran halfway to meet her and others waved their arms for her to run faster. But as she got closer, the crowd grew quiet, as if embarrassed, and the only sounds were the waves and the woman, getting closer, shouting, He's killed him! He's killed him! And the men in the crowd looked at one another and the women looked at the boy in the sand, the trickle of blood looking so thin and weak where it disappeared into the rolling waves at their feet.

Mirta's mother held her hand tight. The crowd stepped aside to let the woman through and they watched as she held the boy's head in her hands. She screamed and sobbed and asked the Virgen how she would dare do this to her, a woman with only one son in the whole world, and some in the crowd shook their heads and looked at the empty sky. And as Mirta watched, the boy slowly stirred. She pointed and her mother moved closer and the woman with the short white hair stopped shouting at the Virgen in heaven and looked back at her boy and now they all stood watching. And when his hand went to his nose and he opened his eyes, the shouting started again. Mirta and her mother were pushed aside as the men picked up the boy and carried him back up the sand. The crowd moved as one with the boy, a screaming, gesticulating mass. And then the whole thing disappeared into one of the round wood houses behind them and the shore was quiet again and all of it had happened so fast that Mirta wondered if she had dreamed it also until she saw the smaller boy in the distance, walking west along the shore.

She stood with her mother where the tide was coming in. They were alone again watching the boy fade like the trees around the bend where the peninsula doubled into itself. Mirta felt a hollow in her stomach and looked to her mother's straw bag. It was still leaning against a tree, a blanket twisted underneath where Mirta had slept. The shade had shifted and half their little camp lay in soft sunlight now. Mirta looked at her mother, who stood still watching the boy.

Mirta's mother walked to the blanket and slowly folded it, her face turned toward the boy, who was now a dot in the distance and not a boy but a memory of one. She picked up the straw bag and slung the blanket over it. She opened her other hand and gestured for Mirta to take it.

"You can keep the photo in your room if you'd like," her mother said.

Mirta jumped suddenly and clapped, the disappointment of the afternoon forgotten for a moment. The photo her mother kept of her father, before he was famous. Propped against her dresser. Just three years old and wearing pants that came to his knees. A little jacket with a round collar. A baseball bat resting sideways against an old tree.

"Can girls be baseball players?" Mirta asked.

After a moment, hearing nothing from her mother, Mirta stopped walking and looked up at her.

"Can I have the photo, really?"

That night, Mirta lay in the narrow bed in the hallway and listened to her mother speak low and fast into the phone and then she lay there long after, listening to the planes fly overhead and imagining the night silhouettes of their wings as they waved forever good-bye to Havana.

The Last Rescue

Anselmo lay next to his wife and tried to think about nothing. The room felt safe and familiar even in the soft darkness that had gathered like drapes in the corners. The shapes and shadows of the night stood where they always had and Anselmo knew this was the dresser, that hulking piece the chair, the figure crouching in the corner only his shoes and cotton pants. The air humming softly through the house was a little cool tonight, though, and he resolved to close the vents a quarter inch in the morning. He turned, pulled the comforter to his chin, and again tried not to think. He moved closer to Meegan, not touching her but close enough so that she would have to touch him if she turned. He lay there and watched her back rise and fall with her breathing. He liked the back of her, liked to watch that sway she put into her walk that was like an invitation full of regrets. He counted her breaths and as he began to grow sleepy, he pushed out that other thought. He mustn't think about it or he would never sleep. Maybe it was just her way of getting back at him for some slight he hadn't even noticed. Maybe she had been brooding for weeks until the moment came for her to say something hurtful. Anselmo couldn't find any other explanation. Not after they had agreed on all the important things for so long. No, he wouldn't think of it. He must sleep. He must sleep immediately. And in the morning, he wouldn't even remember and she would turn to him half asleep and hug him close and he would know she, too, had forgotten. Now he must rest. Tomorrow they were going up again, early. The other pilots would have gotten a good sleep and they would frown at his pallor. Baluti might not even let him go up, ask him how he could spot rafters in the straits when he could barely open his eyes from sleep. That Baluti always knew what Anselmo was thinking. He was afraid of him, thought him some kind of brujo. Anselmo repeated the word to himself—brujo, brujo—until he realized he was still awake. Really, he must think of nothing. He must sleep. This is how his mind began to race and then he would never sleep. Nothing, nothing. Anselmo concentrated on his own breathing, easy and deep.

Meegan turned away, closer to the far edge, and the cold air seeped under the comforter through the new gap. He moved in closer and she turned toward him.

"Meegan?"

Nothing. How did she manage to sleep so well? The first year of their marriage, Anselmo had worried that this easy slumber of hers pointed to some lack in her character. Only children and the simple enjoyed such untroubled sleep. If you were a thinking person, how could you shut your eyes and fall immediately as if under a spell, smile and coo like a baby rocking? How could you help but think of all the things that needed fixing? Later, Anselmo decided that when you are Cuban, you never sleep well. You have suffered more than other people. And he forgave Meegan her simple slumber. But some nights, as he lay there thinking, he had to fight a creeping irritation with her slow breathing. It was as if she had been lying all along. As if she didn't feel anything she claimed to feel and instead vanished every night into a space that was hers alone. If he could only dream her dreams and know. What was it Meegan thought? Why didn't she ever share her dreams in the morning? She told Anselmo she forgot them. Anselmo whose dreams were so alive that he would wake and lie in his sweat sorting out the real from the imagined, trembling at the chasm that had opened in his mind, the vastness of all that lay waiting for him.

Meegan turned onto his arm. Anselmo let himself come under her warmth. He sank back into the bed, easy and soft. He was so fortunate in spite of everything. Meegan who still made the grocery store clerks put down their cans as she walked by. The hazel eyes with their little slant that reminded him of Sophia Loren. His mother had said nothing when he brought her home. When she left she had sighed and said, "Una Americana." Before they were married, his father took him to dinner. A Cuban man can never marry an Americana, he explained. An American man with a Cuban woman, this was possible. She would love him and comfort him like no Americana could, cook hot lunches for him and listen to the details of his day. But an Americana would never understand a Cuban man. She would get angry if you stayed at the table after dinner instead of taking your plates to the sink. She would want you to help her clean, take the broom and sweep out the crumbs from under the table. But Meegan never frowned when, in their early days, Anselmo would lean back in his chair after dinner and open the paper.

So it wasn't she who'd forced him to take on the dishes eventually. He just couldn't bear to see her working. But he never told his father. And when his parents came for dinner, Anselmo leaned back in his chair as before and shared a cigar with his father as if there were nothing more natural in the world. And finally one day his father moved his glass of brandy forward and passed his hand over his face. "I'm happy for you," he said. "For you and Meegan. You're lucky and rare. Two people rarely love each other equally."

Meegan shifted again and Anselmo pulled the comforter up to his chin. The floodlights coming in through the blinds caught the glitter in the textured ceiling and cast soft blue shadows in the room. Like a television broadcasting late into the night, mute and comforting, nothing but blue light and shadows and the hint of glitter stars. Meegan had left her closet door ajar and her clothes hung in straight dark lines. Anselmo turned on his side to see if he could make out her outfits. In the half-light he recognized a long striped dress that she wore when they entertained at home. It was made of a soft knit that rode her curves in a way that was sexy without being cheap. It was Anselmo's favorite dress. He lay quietly, listening to Meegan breathe. The sheet was cool against his chest and he appreciated the heaviness of the comforter. The thermostat clicked off, the hum of the air conditioner now replaced by a tinny echo in his ear. He must sleep. He must.

Anselmo's jeans and T-shirt lay on the dresser, making a mound in front of the mirror. He followed the line of the dresser top across. His wife's perfume bottles stood at the other end, casting their own small shadows in the shiny wood. The mirror reflected the window behind the bed and the gray silhouette of the sapodilla tree, its branches swaying up, down, in long slow dips like an old-fashioned dance, like an old, old dance, down in slow dips, swaying. May I take this dance, my lovely? Yes, of course. Bent low, his arm swaying down, down, down.

"Are you hot?"

"Dance."

"It's hot in here."

"Meegan." Anselmo tucked the comforter under his leg. "I think I was asleep."

"I'm sorry, darling. Aren't you hot?"

Without waiting for an answer, she flung aside the comforter and got out of bed. Her slippers shuffled down the hall. Hush, hush, thought Anselmo, following the sound until it quieted and he knew she was standing in front of the air conditioner. The light in the hall went on, then the shudder of the air and the low moan of its coming back to work. Anselmo realized he had been listening to crickets all this time. Now there was just the moan of the machine. "I'm actually a little cold," Anselmo said when Meegan returned to bed. She pushed his shoulder until his back was facing her and then she cuddled up close to him.

"There," she said. "I'll keep you warm."

Anselmo sank back into his wife's embrace. Her body was soft. Softer than it had been, but in a way that reassured him. The rest of the world had grown rigid, but here was his wife not pretending, just covering him with herself. He began to drift again, but stopped short when he remembered the perfume she had worn. He wanted to describe it to himself. But he realized that after all this time, he still couldn't distinguish the various scents she wore, and Anselmo began to worry about this. What did it mean that he didn't know her perfume? Then just as quickly he tried to put it out of his head. But it stayed back there, prodding him awake each time he began to fade into sleep. She had worn her hair up and dabbed perfume behind her ears. Anselmo had watched her hand around the wineglass as she talked to the new pilot.

But it wasn't that, not really. Anselmo was used to men looking at his wife. True, he had never seen her respond as she had, like a schoolgirl. But didn't he also linger over the round shoulders of salesclerks? Hadn't he hugged Baluti's daughter just a little too long the last time they came back from a run over the straits? These things meant nothing. He was a mature man, a man of the world. No, it wasn't the curve of his wife's fingers on the wineglass that bothered him. It was the conversation. Low and intimate and when Anselmo had moved in to hear, he'd been a little dismayed to learn they were discussing politics. Worse was Meegan's talking in a way Anselmo had never heard. She used to laugh at the way he talked with his hands and once, at one of her family reunions in Maine, she imitated his gestures, exaggerating them in a pantomime that even he found amusing. They're all like that, she said, all the Carillos. And just when he had begun to feel out of place, she planted a big kiss on his cheek and flung her arms around his neck.

But here was Meegan, herself now animated, alive, one hand tight on the glass, the other flying through the air as if it had been charged with saying something she was not allowed to admit.

The air moaned on. Meegan turned in bed. He felt the air on his back and pulled the comforter tighter.

"Meegan? You awake?"

She groaned.

"I heard you talking to him."

"Oh, honey, you've woken me up."

"I'm sorry. I thought you were awake."

Anselmo turned to face Meegan's back, her hair fanned over the pillow, exposing her neck.

He was silent for a long while, trying to think of how to say it. It wasn't a big deal, really. He didn't understand why he would have thought it was a big deal. He would just ask her. And why not? They were husband and wife. He could ask her anything.

"Where did you get that about the embargo?" he asked finally.

Meegan turned suddenly in bed to face her husband.

"You woke me up to talk about the embargo?"

"I'm sorry. No. I was just thinking it was odd, that's it."

"Is that why you're tossing and turning like that? The embargo?"

"Not the embargo. What you said about it."

The room was quiet again. He thought he might have fallen asleep, when suddenly Meegan began to laugh. She reached out and caressed his cheek.

"Do you realize how funny you sound? The embargo, really. Do all Cuban men talk about the embargo in bed?"

Anselmo was quiet. A disturbing image had arisen, Meegan in bed with a slew of Cuban men, ready to test her question.

She moved and Anselmo pulled the sheets to his chin.

"I thought we always agreed that it was the right thing to do, that's all," he said.

Meegan was quiet.

"Meegan?"

"Oh, come on. Don't you have to fly tomorrow? What's gotten into you?"

Meegan turned her back toward him. He had to fly tomorrow. He must sleep. The room shrank around him; the dresser seemed closer than before. The shadow reflection of the sapodilla tree swayed. Branches like arms, thought Anselmo. Spindly arms swaying. How could anyone question that the embargo was the right thing to do? The goods wouldn't go to the people anyway. How could she say it was time to let go? Anselmo shivered. He turned and turned and started to fall. How could they trade with that man? He would blow them up if they went near Cuban waters tomorrow. And why shouldn't they go near Cuban waters? Tell me why not. Who cared what an ancient dictator said on television? Why shouldn't they fly where they wished?

Anselmo woke with a shudder.

"You're talking to yourself," Meegan said and flipped back over.

He lay under the comforter and stared at the glitter in the ceiling. He tried to move closer to Meegan, but stopped before he touched her. Anselmo touched his nose. It was cold and stiff. He turned to the edge of the bed. Should he get out? He tried to remember where he had left his slippers. He peered over the edge of the bed. The white tile gleamed under the night light filtering through the blinds. He must have left them near the bathroom when he took a shower.

"Meegan?"

No answer.

He swung his feet over the edge and slipped from under the covers. On his tiptoes, he scanned the darkened room for his slippers. He'd never sleep now. He was fully awake. Why didn't he ever feel this way those mornings when he had to strap in and take off, knowing for the next three hours he'd be stuck in a cockpit, Mauricio next to him saying, "Go lower, I think I see something." And there was never anything there anymore. What were they doing, really? What was the purpose? They went up day after day and came back with nothing, the U.S. had stopped admitting Cuban rafters anyway. But always Baluti in front of the microphones afterward. The reporters who seemed to be smiling behind their nods. What did it mean? And now to think his wife might be complicating things. Why say that nonsense about the embargo?

He stood in the middle of the room and watched Meegan sleeping. He'd never watched her from this perspective and she seemed smaller, like someone he didn't know. She turned and put an arm out to where he'd be. She needed him. Her dark hair covered part of her face. Anselmo took a look toward the closet and his heart began to beat. It was so dark in there suddenly. Hadn't he been able to see the clothes just a moment ago? He moved closer. Meegan turned and moved toward the edge, one arm over her head now, the other tucked under her. But what was this silliness with the closet? He stepped back and tiptoed to the door. He glanced back again at Meegan sleeping and went out. The hallway was darker than the room and he stood just outside the door a moment to let his eyes adjust. Slowly, details emerged. The lamp at the far end of the living room, its glass dome giving off the slightest night glow. A corner of the dining room table. And at the bottom of the hall, the faint pink glow of the light switch. Anselmo walked quickly, not bothering with his tiptoes now. Without flipping on the light—why wake Meegan?—he felt for the plastic handle on the thermostat and pushed it up. The machine shuddered off with such force that Anselmo took a step back. The quiet hurt his ears, as if a vacuum had entered the house. He stood for a while in the darkness of the hallway. As warmth returned, the quiet filled with small night noises. He heard the crickets again, faintly. And the creak of a soft wind through the rafters. He tiptoed back to the room slowly, alive with every sound of his house.

Back in the room, he stopped in front of Meegan's sleeping figure. The light through the window cast a sheen over her face as if she were shining from within. Her arms were wrapped around her body as in a hug. Her mouth was soft, amused. She lay so still that Anselmo walked slowly to her and crouched near the edge of the bed to be sure she was breathing. He straightened and stepped back. When he turned, he was staring into the dark closet. He could see the striped dress now, an animal hiding in the reeds. He shook his head. He was tired. Dreaming standing up. He turned back to Meegan. She lay in the same position. He faced the closet again and, as carefully as he could, brought the doors together, gently guiding the wobbling edges to a close, and went back to bed. He slipped under the covers and lay still.

Meegan lay on the other end of the bed, turned away from him. She had shrugged the covers off and her bare arm draped over her head as if she were shrinking from some noise. Anselmo traced her silhouette under her thin nightgown.

Mark was the only Americano on their team, a young pilot who had flown in the Gulf War. Anselmo and Meegan had met him two weeks ago at a party Baluti threw for him. Anselmo had danced with Baluti's daughter and afterward sat down with Meegan and Mark. Meegan was sleek and pretty in a black dress and black gloves that covered her elbows, her dark hair gathered loosely over her neck. She wore the necklace he had given her on their wedding day, a diamond obelisk on a short platinum chain. Anselmo had led her through the airy green ballroom, thrilling at the heads that turned so slightly. She fingered her chain as she talked with Mark and the movement sent rainbows of light as if she were giving off sparks.

"We're so glad to finally get a real pilot," Anselmo said, thinking more of the brilliant obelisk, his wife's hand.

Anselmo touched his wife's back. He tried to meet her eyes, but Meegan had turned in a way that no matter how Anselmo tried to get around her, he was always at her back.

Mark looked from Meegan to Anselmo, but only smiled. Meegan continued to turn the obelisk in her hand. Anselmo thought himself spinning, mesmerized by the movement of that gloved hand on the diamonds.

Meegan had stood and held out her hand. "We hope to see you again," she said. And Anselmo made a note of the we, the word filling him with gratitude, Meegan's way of saying that while she appreciated the company, she was part of a whole. But then Anselmo went cold. Was the word really meant to distract him from some truth? He looked to Meegan, who stood with her hands to her side, looking not so much toward Mark as to a point behind him.

When, alone in their bed again, Meegan had caressed him and taken him in her arms, he felt, as he might a real physical sensation, the evening pass into memory. He was tired and alone in himself and afterward he remembered only the way the light had scattered from her hand that night as if she alone had discovered the secret to setting it free. But in the morning she was up before he awoke. And as she poured his orange juice she said they should have a party, invite that new pilot and his wife. Was Mark married, she wanted to know. And in a secret part of himself, Anselmo took note that she mentioned his name four times. Through breakfast, he thought Mark Mark Mark Mark.

Anselmo stared now at the ceiling. Meegan turned and her arm touched his, warm and soft, and Anselmo knew he had made too much of that first meeting with Mark, was making too much of last night's conversation with the new pilot. Here was his wife, a real thing and warm beside him. He moved closer to her, examining her lashes where they met her cheek, soft and downy. But why was she talking to Mark again? A cricket chirped and Anselmo jumped. What was that? Meegan turned over and kicked off the last of the sheet still wrapped around her feet. The cricket stopped. Anselmo loosened his grip on the comforter. Meegan groaned and sat up.

"It's hot in here."

She swung her legs over the edge of the bed and stood. He watched her walk out the door, strong and decisive. He braced himself for the shudder of the air conditioner so that when it came it seemed softer than he had imagined. He listened for Meegan's soft steps in the hallway. But she appeared suddenly in the doorway.

"Did you turn it off or something?"

She got back into bed without waiting for an answer. She lay on her back for a second, then settled onto her side, facing Anselmo, and he thought finally he would sleep. But the chill began immediately, sharper this time, like fingers crawling up from his toes. He moved closer to his wife and wrapped the comforter under his body.

It was June and the days had been beautiful and it occurred to Anselmo that something was wrong. This cold that was so unnatural, these thoughts. He saw the ocean beneath him and him falling, falling out of the sky. The ocean rushing to meet him, the dead rafters signaling from below with their mirrors. Here we are, where we've always been.

A shot. Anselmo sat up. Meegan lay on her side facing away. His heart beat in his ears and he waited, watching, until he saw her back rising and falling. He lay down again and slipped under the covers, waiting for the blood to rush out of his head, for his breathing to quiet. In the darkened room, everything looked blue, as if underwater. The lights sparkled above him like a harbor. In the mirror, a bony hand was shaking its finger back and forth. Anselmo shrank under the covers. He shut his eyes. He must try not to think about anything. What time was it? He wouldn't look at the clock. He turned toward Meegan and rolled himself into a ball. The skin on his arms tingled with goose bumps.

She had stood there, just eight hours ago, with her hand on her wineglass, smiling at the new pilot. "What has the embargo accomplished, really?" she'd said, and the new pilot smiled. Anselmo tried to picture his smile now, but came up with a blank face instead. "It's time to end it," and then she'd turned to Anselmo as if she knew he'd been there all along and added, "Of course, Anselmo would disagree with me."

At first, he'd thought, End what? He knew Mark would go to Baluti later and tell him Anselmo's wife thought we should lift the embargo. The new pilot probably wasn't even thirty, his ideas still rough outlines of the way things ought to be. How could Meegan be so careless? Or was she trying to be careless? It was ridiculous to have these parties before their runs. Baluti's idea: Invite the papers, take photos, The Heroes Celebrating Before the Next Rescue Mission. And what if Fidel did shoot them down over the straits tomorrow? What would it all look like then? A shot and the plane falling. Or the plane falling without a shot? What if it were pilot error? An accident?

Anselmo lay quiet and listened to the moan of the air conditioner. And something else. Something behind it. Moving in the corner. Was that the machine moaning or something else? Anselmo suddenly turned and sat up. There was a figure there. Someone in the room! His wife sighed.

"Meegan, no!" Anselmo cried out.

"My God, you scared me half to death, what's wrong with you?"

Anselmo saw now that it was only his pants and shoes. In the corner where he had left them.

"I'm sorry. I must have been having a nightmare."

She turned without a word. Anselmo moved closer. He wanted to wrap his arms around his wife. Warm and soft. He watched her back rise and fall in the blue light. He was afraid to venture too close to the edge of the bed. Why didn't she turn and take him in her arms again?

"Meegan?"

Anselmo listened to the air conditioner, distinguishing each current that rustled the vent. He must sleep. He opened his eyes. He wanted to be close to Meegan, but he didn't want to look at the closet doors. He turned away. What was she dreaming?

Before they left the party last night, Mark had put a hand on his shoulder.

"Your wife agreed to play tennis with me tomorrow morning," he said. "She says you'll be up in the Piper."

Anselmo replayed it, watching Mark's face, feeling the pressure on his shoulder. Tennis with me. Tennis with me. Yes, he would be up in the Piper in the morning, scanning the straits.

Why hadn't Meegan told him about the tennis? If it was such an innocent thing, why not tell him? Maybe she was waiting to tell him before he left. Maybe she would get up before him and wait in the kitchen, kiss him and mention casually that she was playing tennis with Mark. Meegan was his wife, she loved him.

But she wouldn't tell him. Anselmo had never been so sure of anything before. He knew, the way some people knew that there was a God who cared for them, that Meegan would not get up to say good-bye. That he would dress in the dark, watching her turn in her sleep. It was his fault. That other morning that was too terrible to think about. He must not think about it. Meegan standing by the sink, not saying anything, but not crying either, the blooming memory of his hand on her face, spreading. The shards of glass on the floor. Don't you feel? he had shouted. The whole morning he had thought Mark and the way her lips had formed his name as she poured him orange juice as if it were the most natural thing in the world. When she asked him to bring his plates to the sink, he'd sat for a moment watching her and then kicked the glass, watched as it spun away, bright fragments that caught the light and sparkled, and Anselmo had found it beautiful. "Don't you feel anything?" he screamed. The desire, like an old ache, to feel his hand sharp against her cheek.

This passion of his burned him, tortured him. He was the only pilot who had never spotted a rafter because everywhere he saw her face. And she like a paper flower, turning her head up to receive his kiss, smiling as if lightly amused, as if this weren't love, but a discreet and perfect friendship. And in his mind Anselmo saw what he had been trying not to see. He saw the shards come together and whisper, whole and perfect, that something had broken and it was his fault and it would never be the same again. Two people rarely love each other equally.

Tomorrow he would get in his plane and strap himself in. He and Mauricio would dance figure eights in the sky, Mauricio never once turning to look at him. Anselmo squinting and pretending to see. The water so still that the entire Caribbean would be a mirror on the sun. The brilliance getting inside him, urging him to believe heaven lay at the bottom of the ocean.

Anselmo gave a shudder under the comforter. He opened his eyes and breathed in the cold thin air of the room. The ceiling was littered with broken glass. It distorted the light, sent it running at odd angles. The dresser shone, polished and smooth. And in the mirror, a hand scratched the window glass, one bony finger extended. Anselmo drew closer to Meegan, so close he could smell her. The pile in the corner lay in shadow now, the figure of his last self obscured in darkness.

He had wanted her to scream, to break dishes, to swear and cry and promise to leave, to take everything and walk away. But the days that followed were like the days before. She floated and he reached for her. Finally it was he who came sobbing, begging forgiveness, falling. And now he was falling again. She talking to Mark last night as if nothing had happened. Why hadn't she mentioned the tennis?

Anselmo turned on his back. He brought his arms up from under the comforter. A blue sheen covered them, the hair stood on end. He would get out and walk down the hall and shut off the air once and for all. And then he would sleep. Finally, sweet sleep. He would close his eyes and dream. Anselmo slipped out of the comforter, crouching away from the figure in the mirror. He measured his steps to the edge of the room, letting the cold wrap around him. He stood in front of the door, the knob in his hand, listening to his heart beat a desperate staccato in his ears.

Miami Relatives

My aunt Julia likes to bite people. Usually it only happens when she's angry. But one year at Christmas Eve dinner she got very drunk and right there and then, in front of all those guests who know nothing of what my family is like, she bent close as if to kiss her husband and instead bit part of his cheek off.

People thought it was some kind of show, especially since my uncle was howling a Julio Iglesias tune while his wife had her teeth sunk into his cheek. He ended up needing seventeen stitches.

The scar's still visible after all these years, a white line above his jaw that's like a second smile.

I worry about my family. When I was little I used to lie in bed, unable to sleep, wondering how long it'd be before a giant sinkhole swallowed the house with all of us in it. First would come the noise, like a deep sigh, and then the room would tilt toward the center and all the screaming in the world wouldn't save us. I imagined the hole spreading, taking the Aunt Julia's house next door and then the entire street all the way past the stop sign, moving south from Miami, through the fields and out over the water, eating everything in its path. And then the sinkhole would arrive in Havana and knock on the old uncle's door and wait for him to answer before swallowing him too.

I still think my family would be happiest living underground, blind insects communicating by touch, rubbing antennae, working the same old paths. Every night, I bury them beneath the house. It is a way of keeping them safe.

My grandparents live with us in a little apartment off the back porch. It has a kitchen, but my grandmother refuses to cook in it. She says the spirit of the food will be trapped forever inside her apartment and then she won't be able to sleep at night with all the spirits moaning with melancholy and regret.

So instead, she cooks at the barbecue grill inside the porch, so that the food spirits can escape through the screen. She makes everything there, including her morning coffee, and at least once a week she leaves a pot on to smolder.

My grandmother will go out to the yard and climb the mango tree to have lunch. She'll be sitting there eating out of the bird feeder with the crows and my mother will run out and yell,

"What's the matter with you? What's the matter with you, woman?"

My mother will clap her hands together for attention.

"Look at all this smoke. You're going to burn the house down."

My grandmother has already ruined several good Calphalon pots this way.

In a black closet off the hall, we keep a photo of the old uncle in Havana. The photo is covered with scuff marks and tiny cuts like scratches over his face. Some days you'll pass by the closet and hear screaming. It's hard to invite friends over when you don't know if your mother will suddenly walk out of the closet, her fingernails red with blood.

When my grandfather turned old, a radio grew out of his ear.

Now Radio Mambi follows him everywhere, the high-pitched voices of the afternoon program seeping out of his pores like insects screaming. Even when we all go over to Aunt Julia's to eat, he's there, holding the radio up so it doesn't fall out and take his ear with it. He'll leave the table early and everyone will roll their eyes. When it's time to go, we'll all go looking for Abuelo, and he'll be sitting on the couch, snoring, the radio antenna quivering over his head.

Every night, when he thinks we're asleep, my grandfather calls up the stations that are attached to his ear. Sometimes I'll crawl under my bed and tune in just to hear his voice, the sound of saltwater and sand.

Always, it's the same story about the unbearable heat, about where the breezes hide this time of year. But one night there is something he wants to say about the old uncle in Cuba. He stutters and starts over.

"It's so damn hot in this house," he says instead.

I hear the men on the other end start to laugh and I lie there in the darkness under my bed.

"Damn hot," my grandfather whispers.

On the twenty-sixth of July, the Aunt Julia bites my mother. Bites her on the arms and on the neck. She leaves beautiful red welts like roses. Just as she's about to open her mouth and bite off my mother's nose, Aunt Julia sees me standing there and says,

"Mind yourself, girl. The things that go on in this family are not to be discussed with strangers."

An evil star hangs over our family. This is what my mother tells me one day when the clouds are high and the wind brings relief from the heat. We are cursed from the first pink Gallego who knelt on the white beach down to the old uncle in Havana, who as a boy used to run through the old streets with a loaded gun, screaming, "National pie and friendliness!"

The ghosts of all the dead pursue us still, my mother whispers. They appear at the brightest time of day, when the sun is full in the sky and you are thinking nothing in the world can trouble you. And then the ghost descends in the form of a memory, full of sugar and acid. It pokes the liver and makes the eyes water.

I tell my mother that I know. That I stood outside the Blue Moon one night with the old uncle and pointed a loaded finger at the shiny women.

"National pie!" we cried.

My father comes home from work and sits in his chair. His hair is carefully combed and his tie is loosened. He holds the newspaper in his right hand and after a while opens it and begins to turn the pages slowly. When he's done, he folds it and sets it on the table.

"Ah, world," he says and puts his hands behind his head.

He sits there for a while until he notices and calls me over.

"The real trick in life," he says, "is finding a pink name for sadness."

That night, I tune in to my grandfather on the call-in show.

"I think my son-in-law is dying," my grandfather whispers. "Who will take care of us?"

My mother installs smoke alarms in the porch. Two next to my grandparents' apartment and two more directly over the grill.

"Why'd you do that?" my father asks.

"Mother's going to burn the house down," my mother says.

"But they're directly over the grill," my father says.

"That's the only way they'll go off in time."

"In time for what?"

My mother claps her hands together.

"Look at me," she says. "Don't you know that she's been plotting to burn the house down ever since we moved here?"

One day, my grandmother puts poison in my mother's coffee. Mother drinks it, turns pink, and grows an extra mouth. Through it she smiles at my grandmother. We have such deep love in this family, she says, and opens her arms wide as if for a hug.

I awake in the middle of the night to crashing noises from my grandparents' room.

I walk through the house. I call out for my parents and get no answer.

Another crash. When I reach the porch, I see a light on in the little apartment. I knock on the door. Then I open it.

White plaster dust swirls into my face like snow. When it settles, I see my grandfather standing with a bat in his hands. Behind him, a wide black hole into the night.

"Damn hot in this house," he screams.

My grandmother lies sleeping on the bed, her chest rising and falling on untroubled breaths.

"Damn hot," my grandfather screams again. And we both stand there, the little voices from his radio coming faster and faster like frightened heartbeats.

The Aunt Julia has bitten the mailman because he stole the letter from the old uncle in Havana. She saw him take the letter out of the stack and put it in his pocket. So she waited for him in the azalea bush and when he reached into the mailbox, she jumped out and bit his hand.

"Family is sacred!" she screamed after him.

This is the way it goes around here.

We all pretend to hate the old uncle. But I'm thinking things are more complicated.

Sometimes I think my aunt Julia is really in love with the old uncle. And that is why she waits for him to write. Why she says family is sacred even though she talks all the time about how much she hates him. But when I tell my mother this, she jumps out of her chair and comes after me with the newspaper.

"Devil child," she screams. "Talking what you don't understand!"

And then I stand very still because I'm afraid of the neighbors hearing.

A boy I like has come to dinner. It was his idea. I would never invite anyone to meet my family. But he has come and my grandmother has greeted him at the door wearing leopard-print pants and a tight red shirt that shows her speckled chest. My grandmother kisses the boy and holds the hug until I pull her away. When the boy turns to me, I squeeze his hand hard and his eyes fill with tears.

In the porch, my father is grilling steaks. He wears a soft pink hat that covers his eyes. He drinks a pale milk shake as he turns the steaks. We sit around the table and wait. My grandfather sits there too with the radio in his ear, the antenna waving softly like a third hand.

We talk about everything but the old uncle, though I know it is the only thing my family ever thinks about. The boy who has come to dinner nods and smiles. Every now and then he looks above the grill and then at me.

Suddenly my throat goes cold. All this time the smoke alarm has been blaring and my family has been sitting there talking through it as if it were no more than a whisper in the leaves. Not even I noticed.

My dad finishes grilling the steaks and brings them to the table. My mother forms her lips into a prayer, but all that comes out is the sharp wail of warning.

I am tuned in from my room, listening to my grandfather talk to the radio again. His voice comes over as if from far away.

The radio men chuckle, but my grandfather doesn't hear. He starts and stops and finally sighs and begins his story about the old uncle in Havana. The old uncle had problems in the head because of a family curse, he explains. One day, robbers got into the family home. They came in through a bedroom window and no one heard the glass break until the robbers had filled up two big bags of jewels and money. They would have gotten away, but the old uncle used to sleep under the dining room table. And when the robbers bumped against a chair on their way out, he awoke.

The old uncle grabbed the robbers by the ankles and pulled them to the ground. Then he reached for the pistol he always carried in his back pocket and right there, as the robbers squirmed for mercy in front of him, he shot them dead. Even long after they had stopped moving, the old uncle kept shooting and shooting.

"On windless nights, you can still hear them scream," my grandfather says.

And now he is sobbing and the radio guys are quiet and then the line goes dead and they're playing a Beny Moré song like they do after the soap operas.

The Aunt Julia climbs to the top of the table and holds her arms out for silence.

"Today I ate the sun," she says. "The darkness was delicious."

We sit staring at her until she opens her mouth and blinds us.

After the old uncle shot the robbers in the family home, everyone came running to where he stood in the dining room. The women were afraid he was hurt and covered him with kisses.

My grandmother hung a rosary around his neck. The old uncle reloaded and shot off her thumb.

Then he pointed the gun at everyone.

"Nobody leaves this house," he said.

The hunger became unbearable. They ate the pages of books. They burned suspicious documents for fuel. The old uncle took pity on them. He prepared a feast. Everyone knew he was a kind uncle then.

He built a pit in the living room like our country cousins used to build in the backyard on Nochebuena. He made a spit from young green branches and put the bodies of the robbers on it. My family watched from far away with their fingers in their mouths. The old uncle turned the spit and watched the flames jump.

My aunt Julia took the first bite. My aunt Julia said it was delicious. Then she ran into her room and cried for a month without stopping.

The old uncle went in to comfort her.

For three years, they lived like this. And then at the beginning of the fourth year, the old uncle said anyone who wanted to was free to go. One by one, my family left the house through the back door, leaving everything behind, ashamed of their nakedness.

In my dreams, I am still turning, the heat no worse than a summer blanket that smells of rain.

"Devil child! Talking what you don't understand." My mother is coming after me with the newspaper.

"And what do you think the old uncle did while he was comforting the aunt Julia?

★ ★ ★

My aunt Julia is crying in the azalea bush. I watch her from a distance. After a while she sits and begins to gnaw on her fingers.

"Don't do it," I shout out. My aunt Julia looks at me and I think she is going to start crying again. But instead she opens her mouth.

When I open my eyes again, she is gone and all the azaleas are bleeding as if it were springtime.

The boy I like says that maybe the old uncle wasn't so bad. We are in my house, out in the porch, and he has to whisper because my grandmother has begun to suspect him.

"Maybe the way your family tells it is wrong," he says.

He is a smooth boy, almost hairless, and he sits very lightly on the edge of the chair.

"Maybe," I say.

I am not sure about the old uncle. I have never talked to him or seen him, except for the picture in the black closet.

"Maybe he kicked everyone out of the house because they're all, I don't know, contagious or something." The boy smooths his hair back.

"Or because they were mean to him."

I picture the old uncle sad and alone in his big house. At night he lights a cigar and sits on the roof looking out over the water. Does he think of us? Does he wonder what it's like where we are?

I feel sorry for the old uncle. I do.

★ ★ ★

My mother comes out of the black closet, her face streaked with red.

"Devil child!" she whispers. "He made the aunt Julia scream with the pain."

I am sitting in the porch eating lunch with my grandfather. He takes the sandwich in his long thin fingers. He cuts small bites around the bread, chewing each piece for several minutes. I say I spoke to the old uncle and he told me everything.

My grandfather stops eating and turns his neck toward me. And what did he tell you?

The words are like a spell and now I cannot remember. It was only last night that we spoke. But now I can't be sure that the words I remember are his.

The ancient family house is falling down, I tell my grandfather. The old uncle has sold all the windows for food and when it rains, the house fills with purple shark fish. He has white hair and wears the same uniform he wore when he worked for the railroads. In the daytime he walks around the house giving orders to the four walls. At night he goes out in the street to rescue lame animals. He brings them home and cares for them, and sometimes, to help them, he shoots them dead. He is the most tender of men.

My grandfather listens quietly and then darts out at me, sinks his sharp fingers into my wrists until they bleed.

"Bastard!" he whispers.

★ ★ ★

That night I age a hundred years through the holes in my wrists. The darkness leaves me panting. I am tired from so much walking. I wander through the house for hours until I remember what I am looking for.

I stand outside the closet and listen. After a while I turn the handle. Inside it is dark and damp and cold like the inside of the earth. I light a candle. The old uncle looks down at me with his scratched face, surrounded by black walls. The flickering light makes him jump and twitch and soon I grow nervous too.

We stare at one another.

Finally, when I see day seeping in through the cracks in the door, I bow my head to speak.

"Everyone is wrong," I say. "I can understand the confusion. The boy who loves me is also confused."

I look up at the old uncle.

"You have always known it," I say.

We both begin to laugh. The old uncle has a laugh like an old cat and it scratches my throat.

"There is no curse," I say, and he shakes his head.

And then I don't have to say any more. We both understand everything. There is no curse. There is no bleeding moment when it all began. It is all very simple and funny: He is crazy because of us and we are crazy because of him.

In the morning, the aunt Julia bites off all her fingers.

"Mind yourself, girl," she says. "The things that go on in this family are not to be discussed with strangers."

★ ★ ★

I am squatting with my grandmother in the mango tree, our toes curled around a green branch. My grandmother eats sunflower seeds and throws the pods to the wind. From where we squat, we can see over the tops of the houses with their broken tile roofs and the whirling metal fans that stand like frozen smoke billows. A street runs straight out of the neighborhood south through the orange groves and above it, like a blue strip of light, is the ocean that separates us. I see my grandmother looking out over the water, thinking. She spits out a pod and shifts her weight on the branch.

"We will never be rid of the old uncle," she says, facing the direction of the ocean. "Even after he is dead."

I nod.

"But they say he is very sick," I say.

My grandmother spits.

"The old uncle won't die of any human disease," she says. "The devil himself will come for him on a golden chariot."

We sit on the branch for a long time. Birds come and peck at our hair. They bring twigs for a nest. My grandmother spits out the last of her pods and holds her hands out so the birds can eat her fingers.

My toes hurt where they grip the branch. I wonder how my grandmother can sit here for hours, old as she is. I turn and see her eyes are closed.

"Look," I say and point at a well in the earth. "Open your eyes."

First there will be a noise like a deep sigh and then the house will tilt toward the center and all the screaming in the world won't save us. Aunt Julia's house will disappear too and the fields beyond it, all the orange groves and the green grass and the houses with broken tile roofs and the street that goes straight out of the neighborhood.

"Everything will sink and we'll be forced to live under the earth," I tell my grandmother. "Each generation more blind than the last until a thick layer of skin covers our eyes."

Now the family has gathered under the tree and they are screaming up at us.

"Devil child!" my mother says and claps her hands.

"Mind yourself, girl," says the aunt Julia.

The antenna growing out of my grandfather's ear quivers.

They shake their fists up at us, but my grandmother does not move. She sits in the mango tree with her toes curled around the branch. She will not open her eyes and I try to wake her, but my voice is thin and small as a grasshopper's.

"He is crazy because of us," I whisper. "And we are crazy because of him."

The Party

The old woman is at his ear again, a jumble of half-forgotten words until she whispers, "But have we been here long?"

Ernesto squeezes her hand and smiles before nudging past her.

"Not too long, not too long," he says, but his thoughts are already elsewhere. A woman Ernesto recognizes is walking through the front door and he makes his way to her.

The restaurant's bare bulbs are covered tonight with paper lanterns that cast crosses of light across the tables. Streamers hang from the ceiling. Members of the band Máximo hired stand around in a corner, lights reflecting in their shiny suits. Ernesto stops by the door and smiles at the young woman who stands looking out into the restaurant.

"Oh," he says and pauses. "Mirta."

The young woman looks at him and laughs.

"Oh," she says. "Ernesto. Did I disappoint you?" Her eyes turn down at the corners and when she smiles a dimple forms in her left cheek.

Some recollections fade; others continue to sharpen in shadows until one day, suddenly, they prick through the veil of years. Standing there in front of that young woman, Ernesto could not be certain of where in time he stood. And for the first time in his life he wondered how often he had been misled by a familiar gesture, fallen in love again with a memory.

"You look so much like your mother," he says.

"Yes," Mirta says. "Everyone says that."

She kisses Ernesto on the cheek.

"Is he here yet?"

Ernesto shakes his head, aware that he is still holding her hands.

Máximo had called Ernesto before anyone else.

"Joaquin is coming," he'd said simply. It was just like Máximo. He didn't need to say all the rest. He didn't need to tell Ernesto that much time had passed; that Joaquin, too, had paid for the vanished years. With Máximo, the truth came bare and neat.

When Ernesto didn't respond, Máximo cleared his throat.

"I'm throwing a party for him at the restaurant," Máximo said. "I hope you'll come."

Ernesto was silent for a moment. He knew that his hands on the phone were cold and stiff.

"A party for Joaquin Rivera," Ernesto said.

After Máximo hung up, Ernesto lay on his couch and stared at the ceiling. It had never occurred to him that it was a different shade of white from the walls and Ernesto bent his head back and forth trying to decide if it was a trick of the light.

He didn't sleep. But as he lay there, an image began to form in Ernesto that was very much like a dream. It happened more and more, these images that bubbled into his consciousness as if his collected memories had grown too vast to be contained.

Ernesto and Máximo with Joaquin on the bus to Varadero. Late afternoon, the sun coming in sideways through dusty windows. The slow bus straining through its rocking, the broken light mottling blank faces. They have their swimsuits, are going to dive for lobster and later sail out toward the darker waters. The others singing. But Ernesto is sure that he will die before the night. That the light patches are the day's final gift to him. A young man and already wondering which way his ghost will fall.

He stands on the landing watching Joaquin bound ahead, life enough for the three of them.

This is how it was before politics and leaving; this is the image that Ernesto rubs like an amulet against the others.

They called him El Alemán, because only the Germans who vacationed in Varadero were pinker or stronger. You could see the veins bulging in his hands and under the pale white skin of his forearms. Joaquin filled the room he rented with copies of books no one had ever heard of. Poetry books in Persian and Urdu, homemade books bound in red ribbons. He was the only one who got involved with the student movement, organizing marches to the capital, talking about the man who was going to save the country. Even then Ernesto thought Joaquin was campaigning for a version of himself. The leader and the student even looked like the same man. People listened to them the way they had listened to their fathers.

Ernesto stands by the door. He looks at his watch and when he looks up, Hortencia is standing in front of him, balancing a plate of food. She is round and her face is lined. But she stands with one foot slightly in front of the other, her free hand turned up gracefully, an echo of someone she might have been.

"I hope Máximo doesn't mind if I start eating," she says without greetings. "If I wait for Joaquin, I'm liable to just faint."

Ernesto nods and tries a smile. Hortencia holds up her fork.

"You know, Ernesto," she says and pauses to chew. "Well. I was just going to say that I didn't expect you here."

Ernesto looks at her steadily. Then he shrugs, decides not to answer, and rocks back on his heels. "And you," he says. "I didn't know you knew Joaquin so well."

Hortencia narrows her eyes at him.

"You wouldn't know this, of course," she says, bending in closer, "but Joaquin was *very* much into the theater." She raises an eyebrow and nods gravely. "Oh yes, he was," she says. "I knew him before all the politics. He didn't start up with that until after Felipe and I left for Miami."

She looks at Ernesto. She smiles and gives a little bow when Ernesto nods. "Well, he was the most marvelous of performers—what a future this guy had. You should have seen him." Hortencia opens her eyes wide.

When Ernesto first met her, he thought she had a certain grace—a good humor which, especially in the early days of exile, he found captivating and fresh. Nothing seemed to get her down. Oh darling, even bad news was just a passing thing. But as Ernesto came to know her over the years, at the annual parties, the weekend barbecues, Hortencia's wide gestures and high voice began to seem as artificial as smiles in a painting.

"I'll bet he was something onstage," Ernesto says.

"Mi amor, he was *more* than something," Hortencia says. "That big man had the lightest voice of all of God's angels."

Hortencia reaches behind her to set the plate on a table and sighs. Then she spreads both her arms above her and begins to sing in a deep and clear voice.

Ernesto cannot place the melody, but the way the final notes turn downward takes him to a younger part of himself and he knows the song is trying to make him recall some unpleasantness. He notes Hortencia's closed eyes, her smudged lipstick. Ernesto reaches out to touch her, and she brushes him off. She stops singing, turning her back on a smattering of applause.

"He sang it much better, of course," she says quietly. "He would have been one of the great ones, you know. But his parents forbade it."

She holds her hands to her chest and pounds it as the women used to in church.

Ernesto glances at the front door. Several more people have come through and he doesn't recognize any of them. Across the room, the old woman who follows him everywhere holds her hand out as if to get his attention, show him that she's still there. Ernesto makes a motion with his head, then turns back to Hortencia. He touches her arm.

"But look at you," Ernesto says. "You haven't changed in twenty years. I don't know how you do it—always the diva."

Hortencia frowns. "You think at my age I still fall for flattery," she says. "You weren't listening to anything I said."

"Of course I was and of course you look great."

Hortencia looks at him and, after a moment, tilts her head into a pose.

"We would have all been in a much better place if Joaquin had stayed in the theater," she says. She looks at Ernesto a long time. "All of us."

Ernesto nods, watches Hortencia go. The song she sang, he remembers it now and that year that everyone sang it. He remembers Joaquin humming it, and his own brother too. But his guilt is so old that he is comfortable in it; it is a warm hole.

The old woman finds him in the half-light under a paper lantern. She wants to know who has brought her here. She whispers so as not to offend the family: "Tell me again who is it who has died?"

Ernesto stops, turns to go. But instead of walking, he leans back toward the old woman and talks directly into her ear. "No

one has died, Señora. No one. Only Joaquin has finally come
out of Cuba."

Ernesto steps away and the old woman nods.

"El Alemán," she says. And then, quietly, "El asesino."

The flight is a late one and Ernesto worries that no one thought
he might be too tired for a party. But the more he stands there
thinking about it, the more he thinks he'd rather see Joaquin
tired. Not so much as deflated. Just tired enough to smooth
the old roughness. Ernesto sits by the door. He wants to be the
first to see Joaquin. He has decided he will hug him. And then
he thinks of a story he heard: of two men who were no longer
friends or enemies, joined only by the same frail history. When
they met again in exile, they hugged each other with such fe-
rocity that they broke three ribs between the two of them.

Ernesto looks up each time the bell on the door sounds, searches
for a face he recalls, sometimes even stands and shakes hands.
He thinks of what he will say to him. The call of the party is a
low hum that spikes now and then, a bulge of laughter and then
smooth and glassy. Ernesto stands and begins to pace.

He feels a squeeze to his shoulder and turns. Máximo is
smiling up at him.

"What do you think?" he says. "He'll be impressed, yes?"

"It's a surprise?"

Máximo nods. "He thinks he's just picking up something
to eat."

"But it's so dark in here."

"Part of the surprise," Máximo says. "Don't be so glum."

Ernesto waits for a moment before speaking. He is thinking of what Máximo is thinking.

"You think he is the same?"

"The same. What does that mean? Same, same, same. Of course people don't remain the same," Máximo says. He looks at Ernesto.

"So you think that people change."

Máximo is staring off. He shrugs. "I don't think so," he says. "They just get older, realize some things."

Máximo stops himself and looks at Ernesto. They stand side by side. The restaurant has grown noisy toward the front where some of the younger people sit around a big table sipping drinks with umbrellas.

"You know what I was remembering the other day?" Ernesto says. "That trip we took to Varadero."

"Which trip?"

"One of the last ones. To dive for lobster."

"When the police stopped us."

"Not the police," Ernesto says, "some tipo from the hotel."

Máximo nods his head slowly and then smiles. "And there I stood with a suitcase full of squirming lobster."

Ernesto laughs. "Thank God for Joaquin."

Máximo shakes his head. "What do you mean, Joaquin? Thank God for you."

"But Joaquin faked the epileptic attack."

"It was you who had an attack," Máximo says and laughs. "A real one. Asthma or something. You stopped breathing and we had to get the hotel medic to give you a shot of something."

Ernesto stops and looks at Máximo. "You have it all wrong."

"You have it wrong, my friend," Máximo says. He claps him on the shoulder. They stand together a moment and then Máximo waves to someone across the room and begins to walk away.

"Why don't you help yourself to some food, eh?" he says as he goes. "Might be a while."

Ernesto shakes his head. Máximo cheery and businesslike. And for him to have forgotten the details of the last good memories between the three of them. It wasn't like him at all.

"Thank you," Ernesto says. "You're right."

The tables have been pushed to the sides to make room for dancing, though except for a few practice notes, the band has done little more than watch the crowd as if they were the entertainment. The restaurant is loud from shouting and laughter. People have gathered into protective clusters. In the corner, Raúl and Matilde are motioning to Ernesto.

"What were you and Máximo talking about," Raúl says when Ernesto reaches his side.

"Old stories," Ernesto says.

"Did he tell you he's thinking of selling the restaurant?"

"Máximo would never sell the restaurant," Ernesto says.

"Rosa's been pretty sick," Matilde says.

Ernesto thinks. "He didn't say anything about that. The restaurant or anything about anyone being sick."

Raúl offers Ernesto a cigar. "Awful sad."

"What is it?"

Raúl shakes his head. Matilde mouths the word and Ernesto catches it silently: cancer.

They stand and after a while, Raúl says, "I think it was good of you to be here."

"How could I not come," Ernesto says.

"I didn't say anything about you not coming, just that I'm glad you're here."

Matilde points her chin across the restaurant.

"Remarkable how that girl looks like her mother."

Raúl bends down to spit into a flowerpot.

"Nah," he says. "Her mother was much more beautiful."

Raúl smiles at Ernesto before shouting over the crowd: "Hey, beautiful. Why don't you come over here and brighten the evening for two tired old men."

From across the room, Mirta turns. She bends forward to see and then waves at their little group.

Ernesto looks at Matilde. She is looking ahead, her face smooth and impassive.

The old woman walks through the restaurant alone. She stops and points to an areca in a red ceramic pot.

"In Cuba," she says, "we used to put iron spikes through the guanabana trees. They gave the biggest fruit that way."

They don't talk, just watch Mirta walk toward them. Matilde is the first to draw her near for a hug.

"Hello, cariño," she says and caresses her hair. "What are you doing wasting your evening with a bunch of old people?"

Mirta smiles. "Now, if I answered, I'd be calling you old, wouldn't I?"

"Just like her mother," Raúl says.

"Why didn't she come?" Ernesto says.

"She's in North Carolina," Mirta says. "Sometimes Miami's too much for her. But she wanted me to give her love to Joaquin."

"Yes," Matilde says, "of course."

Raúl looks at Matilde and points a finger at her. Ernesto worries that he will say something, but then there is loud shouting from the front of the restaurant and they all turn. Matilde touches her husband's arm.

"Joaquin!" she says.

Raúl shakes his head and holds up his hand. "No, it's not."

A woman's voice silences the rest of the crowd.

"Don't call hijo de puta someone who is helping change things."

Matilde opens her eyes wide at Ernesto. "Is that Máximo's daughter?" she whispers.

He holds a finger to his lips. Another woman is shouting now and knows she has an audience: "You were a little child when that man came to power. I carried you in my arms. And now look at you. A grown woman and that man is still running our country. I carried you in my arms!"

Other people are shouting and Máximo comes out of the kitchen wiping his hands.

"Oye! Oye!" he's saying. And then the individual voices are swallowed again in the low hum of resumed conversations.

"Who was she talking about?" Matilde says.

"Who?"

"Máximo's daughter. I hope she wasn't saying what I think she was saying."

"No, no, of course not," Mirta says. "She was talking about dissidents, in Cuba. We've been talking about it, the risks that they take."

Raúl lets out a groan. "There is no such thing as dissidents in Cuba. You think Castro has lasted forty years by letting people speak their minds?"

"So what are you saying, then?" Mirta says. "That these people are frauds?"

"I'm saying, don't be naive, little girl."

"Now, Raúl," Matilde says, "that's not nice."

But Mirta is smiling. "Well, I remember very little of Cuba, it's true. But what about Joaquin?"

Matilde looks at Ernesto before speaking. "Joaquin's case is special," she says.

Raúl interrupts her. "Look, more than anything, Joaquin was a kind of—how would you say it here?—a ladies' man."

Matilde shakes her head at Mirta.

"What are you talking about?" Raúl says. "At the University, he always had someone's boyfriend coming after him. I used to hide him in my room. Everyone knew where he was. But it gave folks a way out of the unpleasantness, you understand."

Raúl takes a drag on his cigar and lets out a puff of laughter.

"Though I remember one time, one time he almost didn't make it. Ay, ay, ay. That Joaquin," Raúl says and wipes his eyes.

"He comes running into my room. It must have been way past midnight and I was reading in bed—the University was still operating then. And suddenly there's Joaquin, whispering, 'Oye, chico, tremendo lio,' and he disappears into the bathroom down the hall. Before I could say anything, there's a guy standing in my doorway. He's about as big as Joaquin and it's so late and I'd already had so many problems with the landlady."

Raúl takes a long last drag and throws his cigar down, putting it out with his shoe so he can tell the story with both hands.

"So I get really serious. Ask him who the hell he thinks he is." Raúl stops and opens his eyes wide. "Imagine that," he says. "Imagine me lying there about to be shot."

He turns to Mirta. "This was no small thing," he says. "All the students carried guns back then."

"Yes. I know."

Raúl wipes his forehead. "Anyway, I'm getting a little worried when I hear, from the bathroom down the hall, a door cracking open and then a woman's voice—a somewhat deep woman's voice—saying, 'Ernesto, mi amor, who's bothering us at this time of night?'"

Raúl slaps his thigh and shakes his head. "Oh God. It took everything I had to answer in a very serious voice, 'Don't worry, Violeta, it's someone with the wrong room.'"

Ernesto laughs, but Matilde says, "Violeta, eh?"

"Oh, come on," Raúl says. "It was the first name that came to mind. It's a good thing I didn't call him Joaquina."

Mirta rolls her eyes.

"I don't know about that story," she says with a smile. "It sounds like something you saw in a movie."

Raúl shrugs. "You don't understand. This guy was an original." He turns to Ernesto. "You know, he told me once that he spent his entire wedding reception kissing the bridesmaids behind the bandstand."

Matilde, who has been looking at the floor, suddenly blurts out, "He asked me for a recipe once."

There is a long silence when it seems everyone at the restaurant has stopped talking. And then Raúl lets out a long laugh.

"Maybe you didn't know him as well as you think you did," Matilde says. "He liked to bake when he was upset."

Raúl turns to his wife. "I'm sorry, honey," he says and coughs for breath. "You don't need to sound so defensive. I thought you were making a joke."

He turns to Ernesto. "See," he says, "even Ernesto is laughing."

"Well," Ernesto says, holding up his hands, "I'm not sure he was much of a romantic hero either. I think most of his conquests were in his own mind."

Ernesto catches Matilde's smile and wishes he could squeeze her hand.

"Well, none of it sounds like the man my mother described," Mirta says. "I imagined him serious and troubled by—"

Raúl interrupts her. "Nah, nah, troubled!" he says and begins to talk again, fast and nervous. But Ernesto stops hearing. He sees the old woman by the areca and the way she is standing alone and fragile makes Ernesto think of his own mother. He knows the day has been too long for him and he is a little sorry he came, sorry he has let himself get too tired to hold back the images in his mind.

He tells his mother to go away, but she won't move. After all these years, she's still sitting by the window at the farm, the light washing her face until it glows against a backdrop of stars. The island is rotten from before the time of the Spanish, she says. The murdered Siboney go on breathing beneath the Sierras, stirring up winds, spawning the hurricane men.

It all happened so long ago, Ernesto says. You have to forget it now. But his mother shakes her head, goes on spinning stories from the night breezes, her bare fingers working an invisible thread. Your brother is only away on a trip to the capital, she tells him. He will return thin and hungry and I will feed him. In a few weeks we'll get a postcard. You'll see.

The old woman sees him staring and shouts across the room. "There are no dissidents left anywhere, not even here," she says. "Don't you see how all the radio stations have gone to cooking and religion? No one talks about politics anymore."

The woman pauses and comes closer so she can lower her voice. Ernesto stands for what seems like hours waiting for her to reach his side.

"I think Castro came to Miami dressed as a banker and bought them all up," she whispers. "That's what I think."

Raúl is still talking when Ernesto turns to Matilde and says, "Do you think that people change?"

Matilde looks at him in surprise and, after a moment, she shrugs. "You worry about different things," she says. "The things that always bothered you, one day you wake up and they don't bother you anymore."

Ernesto nods. "Or you become so comfortable with them that you stop noticing."

Raúl stops talking and frowns. "What are you two talking about?"

"I think Joaquin," Matilde says. "Am I right, Ernesto?"

Mirta touches Ernesto's arm. "How did you know Joaquin?"

Ernesto watches as Mirta brushes her hair off her shoulders. He sees now that she is not very much like her mother. Her hair is lighter and her nose is thin and upturned. Her question is full of the empty politeness the young show the old. It sits like candy in a pretty bowl.

"Not very well," Ernesto says and tries a smile. The others look at him and then into their hands. Ernesto guesses it is almost midnight.

"He was a big man; we called him El Alemán," he says. He wonders about the stories the others told and looks around the room.

"We had a friend in common back from the time we were students." Ernesto pauses to put his hands in his pockets. "Both of them were—well, both of them opposed the dictator."

He speaks slowly, as if a younger self were dictating the story to him. "And these two young men were very strident about what they believed because they were young and frustrated and Cuba was Cuba, slow and languid in everything but politics, you see."

The paper lanterns lengthen Raúl's shadow along the floor and Ernesto wonders what the light is doing to the figure of himself. Could people warp under the lights like shadows?

"This friend we had," Ernesto says, "he's dead now. He died very young.

"But as a young man, he was very involved in the movement. So much so that when his own brother began typing up leaflets that he didn't like, this friend—well, this friend called on Joaquin, you see. Joaquin was rising in the system pretty quickly—he was tall, as I said, and pink and handsome and everyone is seduced by those things."

Ernesto gives a smile. "Even revolutionaries are seduced by those things." He takes his hands out of his pockets and looks at them. "This friend only went to Joaquin for advice. Joaquin went to another friend for advice. And so on. No one blamed Joaquin, especially since a few months later, the revolution came for him as well."

Ernesto looks at Mirta. "You will see. The bad that happens, happens suddenly."

He remembers how his mother held conversations with his brother through the night. Sometimes laughing, looking down at her lap. Other times she stood and screamed at the slanting light, the flat door. And Ernesto sat on the floor looking back at her. This is how it is in his memory, him sitting at his mother's feet for days, without food or water, fed by their waiting. And

Ernesto waiting with her, though he knew. Wondering if some-day he would see his mother again and tell her the truth and kill both her sons for her at once.

Through his old thoughts, Ernesto hears Raúl connecting words without meaning: tough times, idealism, the struggle, disap-pointment. And Matilde with the aggressive empathy of pow-erless women following right behind him, scattering pretty words like rice at a wedding. All around him, the party swells with phrases and pieces of words, snatches of breath and insults and declarations of love.

Suddenly, Ernesto is weary of language, weary of words and the memories they try to trap and kill for viewing. He is tired of all the layers in a sentence, the phrases that live only to conceal.

"Talk, talk, talk," he says. "No more talk."

The others don't seem to notice him.

He thinks now, old as he's become, that he would like to welcome blankness, to live in a white house with white walls and white floors. He would banish films and photographs, ev-erything that dulls the moment with yesterday's thin light.

He thinks he could pin a single truth to the wall and force himself to memorize it.

He looks at the others, their faces as unchanged as a can-vas, their mouths moving up and down, chewing or talking, Ernesto can't be sure.

"My brother died in jail," he says.

He sees Mirta make a move toward him and he stops her.

Twenty years from now she will remember this moment and think of the right words and be sorry that she didn't say them. Only much later will she know it was best to say nothing at all.

Máximo walks to the middle of the restaurant and holds his hands up for silence. "The plane was late coming in," he says. "It won't be long now."

There is a sprinkling of applause and then silence. The door is locked against the night, Eighth Street not being what it was. The waiters are up again, straightening aprons, restacking the silverware. Their faces in the long mirror are smudged with fingerprints.

Ernesto moves to the door, watches the quiet street.

The old woman who follows him everywhere is at his ear again, pulling the edge of his sleeve as she whispers, "Tell me again why I'm here?"

The light up the block turns to red and a row of cars collects behind it. Maybe Joaquin is in one of them. Maybe he has moved the seat back because his big heavy legs are folded uncomfortably. Or maybe he has already walked through the door so thin and small that no one has recognized him and he is roaming the room even now, listening to familiar lies, remembering faces by the stories they tell.

Ernesto turns to the old woman.

"You see, Señora," he says. "We've been in this country for almost forty years."

Her Mother's House

The road to her mother's house crossed a wooden bridge into a field of sugarcane that bent green and wide to the horizon before it narrowed into a path flanked on both sides by proud stands of royal palms. It was a late afternoon in summer and the men were coming in from the fields, hauling their machetes behind them. They stepped aside with their backs against the palms to let her pass and then stood waiting for the dust to settle, their hats flopping softly in the breeze. Lisette watched the men in the mirror until they retook the road and then her eyes were on the green fields ahead of her, the blue hills that dipped over the edge of sky. The thick warm air curled through the open window and the uneven road bumped her along in a seamless and predictable rhythm. She hummed a tune she had heard last night in the hotel and then she was silent, listening to the palm wind, the road beneath the wheels. It was the first time she had been alone in years and the new quiet seemed something she could touch, an opening in her chest that was as real as her childhood faith.

~

She was born in Miami, two years after the revolution. Her parents had met waiting in line at the Freedom Tower and married just two months later. He was a young student from Oriente, who'd come fleeing Batista. She was from a wealthy landowning family outside Varadero, who'd come fleeing Castro. For years, Lisette thought Batista Castro was one man, the all-powerful tyrant of the Caribbean, the bearded mulato who shot poor workers in the fields and stole her mother's house with all her photographs in it.

That house. Always in the air, behind every reproach. Her mother half mad with longing. And that winter morning when Lisette thought she began to know her mother. Twelve years old. Reading alone in her room, she heard the sobbing before she saw that her mother had crawled in on her knees, a long end of toilet paper in her hands.

"Look at this, feel how soft this is," she cried, holding out the paper to Lisette. "In Cuba today the little children have to use whatever scraps of paper they can find in the trash, bits of newspaper, cardboard. Oh, feel how soft this is."

Her mother had let her body drop to the floor and she lay there for a long time, shredding the paper into smaller and smaller pieces. Lisette sat at the edge of her bed, watching and waiting for her father to come in the room and gently lift her mother. She had turned to Lisette, her eyes open wide.

"When the soldiers came for the house, I walked straight, not turning once to look at the stained-glass windows," she cried softly now. "Not even the white columns that climbed to the second floor."

And the iron railing on the balcony where the rattan furniture was laid out for company, the clink of glasses. Lisette began to remember all of it too.

Lisette married a round-faced boy whose parents were from Varadero, a short drive from her mother's hometown. They each needed someone to agree with. After everything, she still kept the photo that made it into the society pages, Lisette smooth-faced and skinny in the billowy dress, Erminio's arm wrapped tight around her waist, as if already he worried she was a wisp of smoke, a thin memory of herself.

She was a new reporter, covering city hall and trying to find a world within the small concerns of small towns, the wider life in berms and set-asides. He was a young lawyer who hated the law and preferred to make poems out of her stories. Every Sunday, he recited his creations in a deep sleepy voice:

The
Sweetwater city council
today
approved pre-
liminary plans for a new
shopping center on
the
corner
of
Eighth Street and
107th Avenue.

The first months, he waited for her to wake. He poured her the orange juice and the coffee and read her his newspaper poems. Some mornings, when the night's images had vanished, she would kiss him. And they would return to the bedroom and he would whisper her breath back to her.

Later, she began to linger in bed alone, waiting for him to go. Even after they stopped talking, he'd leave a poem by the toast. Paint a heart. Some mornings she could still smell him in the kitchen and her heart would turn.

At lunch she would take a sandwich and sit alone by the bay, imagining the stories in each ripple of water, each cloud that had the strength to push across the sky.

One Christmas Eve she sat apart from Erminio as she had for months and watched him with the women. He said something and they giggled, clapping their hands together like little girls playing at tea. How they loved him, his long frame and freckled skin. They sat in a circle around the pool, under the lights her father had strung from the second-floor balcony to the roof of the gazebo. It was one of those clear December nights that Lisette still loved about Miami, everything clean. One of her cousins produced a guitar and began to sing a bolero, a soft and sad contemplation behind the notes. The applause was slow. Her cousin's father took the guitar away. "Playing sad songs on Christmas, what kind of musician are you?" and he began to strum out an old danzón. Erminio stood and walked to where she was. He sat next to her, took her hand. He squeezed it. She looked at the pool, at the ripples of light.

"It makes me afraid," he said. "How much I need you."

Lisette moved her head with the music.

"It's true," he said. He squeezed her hand. She looked at him and he squeezed harder.

"You're hurting me," she said. "What's the matter with you?" She stood. The music stopped and the others looked up. Erminio sat staring down at the ground, his shoulders bent a little toward his chest. His right hand shook. "Can't you leave me alone for one minute?" Lisette whispered at him. "One minute."

It was terrible the way he kept believing that history would reignite the now. He really thought they could be like they were. Not just them. Everything. Everybody. It made Lisette want to scream. The past wasn't something you could play again like an old song.

Erminio got up and walked to the far end of the yard, falling away from the gazebo lights. Fine, go, she said. And already Lisette was regretting the night.

There were moments that seemed, in their first rush of happiness, strong enough to outrun the inevitable. The night in Isla Mujeres, the wet breeze and the call of fishermen. They had lain skin to skin, remembering, Lisette watching the reflected water draw patterns on the wall. Later, when he went down to phone his parents in Miami, she had wrapped herself in the blanket and slipped away to the terrace off the hallway to smoke a cigarette. She saw him return to their room. She watched him shut the door. She waited until the door flung open again and she saw Erminio pause in the hallway, his face gray. He turned toward the next room, as if listening. He passed his hand over his face and then made a sudden run for the stairs. She stepped out and called after him. He looked up and saw her. He ran back and swept her in the air. She cried. She wanted so badly to love him.

And then Lisette was in the back roads of Cuba thinking it had been so long since she'd been alone.

~

The green fields turned yellow and then brown. Lisette had set out from Havana in the early morning, but now the day was stiffening, the light falling in heavy sheets that made the loose gravel shimmer in the distance. She had been driving for more than five hours and the feeling began to creep on her that she had made a wrong turn somewhere.

But she drove on, the road desolate except for the royal palms that were so much like the stories she remembered. Her mother had shut her eyes when Lisette told her she was going to Cuba. It was a simple reporting trip, a stroke of luck. She wasn't going to explain to her mother things she could barely explain to herself. How every story needed a beginning. How her past had come to seem like a blank page, waiting for the truth to darken it.

Her mother had frowned. What kind of paper sends a young woman to Cuba alone, with the rafters churning more and more chaos. She had bent in closer and looked Lisette in the eyes. After a moment she had leaned back and put her hands in her lap. She wouldn't find the answers to her failures there, if that's what she thought. The remark had cut into Lisette. But she pretended not to understand. Maybe her mother could give her a map to the old house? Cuba's changed, it's not the Cuba I was born in, her mother had said. And then finally, It's a mistake for you to go now. The now was deliberate. And Lisette recognized it as part of the sentence her mother left unsaid: Now that you're divorced. Her mother had taken it hardest. Her family weren't failures. In the end, Lisette promised to go without the map or her mother's blessing. She knew the house was outside Varadero, near Cárdenas. She would find it on her own.

At the airport, her mother had parked and walked her to the terminal. Her face was puffy.

"So you're going."

Lisette nodded. Her mother hugged her and took her hand. She pressed a note.

In Havana, Lisette had worn her mother's map smooth, like tissue paper. The names had changed, but the streets remained. The Malecón still faced toward Miami even after all these years. On every old street, the billboards insisted on the revolution. "We defend the right to happiness" and "The revolution is eternal." Lisette thought back to her marriage. The reassurances built upon their own disintegration. The more they said I Love You, the more they knew it was an empty incantation. Still, she thought she had been right to come. The people had been kind. The police hadn't followed. In the mornings, when everything was fresh and new, she had thought that they had something here that her parents' generation had lost in exile. The feeling evaporated by the end of the day, replaced by a watery feeling that she would never understand herself, much less this country that seemed intent on killing itself slowly. And before she fell asleep each night, despair took her again.

The road curved and the fields were green again and the blue hills were visible to the south. A man approached on horseback, growing in relation to the hills with every step. She pulled to the side of the road and examined her mother's map. On the lower right-hand side, her mother had painted a large box and labeled it simply, M. Lisette looked outside at the expanse of palms and orange trees. Her mother and her cryptics. She was probably afraid Lisette would be stopped with an incriminating document. Lisette got out of the car and sat on the bumper to wait for the man. The afternoon was hot, but the air smelled of oranges as if it were dawn. Now and then a weak breeze moved through and made a sound in the grass. The man got closer, filling up more and more of the sky, until he was upon her and Lisette sat waving her soft map like a small flag.

The man took off his hat and nodded, as if unsure he would be understood. It had happened to her in Havana and

Lisette had been vaguely hurt that no one recognized her as Cuban.

"Buenas tardes," Lisette said, exaggerating the contours of the words so the man would have no doubt she was one of them.

He smiled. "¿En qué la puedo ayudar?"

Lisette showed him the map and pointed at the road that was supposed to lead to her mother's house. She pointed to the block in the right-hand corner, where the road branched to the right. She looked up.

"Militar," the man said and shrugged as if something struck him as silly. The notion of a military base in the middle of the campo? Her mother's precautions?

He took the map and studied it. Then he turned it upside down and nodded, smiling, to point where she was. If she continued this way past the small cane refinery and turned right on the first main road, she would pass the military installation on her right. Then if she took the first left, she should get to where she wanted to go. No photos at the military installation. He handed the map back. They'll take your camera.

Thank you, she said. "Gracias."

The man put his hat back on and watched her for a moment before returning to the road.

The military base looked deserted, but as she got closer, Lisette noticed one soldier standing in the middle of the road. She slowed. He was very young and held his rifle carelessly. She gripped the wheel as she came up beside him. Suddenly, he took a step out of the way. Lisette heard herself take a breath. The boy knocked his feet together and saluted. Lisette stared for a moment, then smiled. She thought of waving and decided instead to nod as she passed the boy. Surrounded now by the wet green of the countryside, Lisette doubted anyone had either the inclination or the money to follow anyone else. It was as if the whole country had agreed to stop caring. Only Miami still cared. And that made Lisette feel an unexpected pang for her parents. She took a left at the road the old man had told her to and began to rehearse what she would say to the people living there now. Apologies, of course: I can go away if you want. I only needed to see my mother's old room. Upstairs, near the back, the one with a balcony with an iron railing and a view of the rose garden.

If they let her, Lisette would take pictures for her father. Show him the lost space from where his wife had emerged, naked except for her stories. The first years of their marriage, all her mother did was talk about her lost plantation. Her father told Lisette how she used to lie in bed giving him imaginary tours of the house. The graceful stairway laced with gardenias in the summer, the marble fireplace her father had installed on a whim after visiting the States, the long white-shuttered windows that looked out over the gardens, the mar pacíficos, the royal palms. Your grandfather was the only one who could grow roses in Cuba. People came from as far as Oriente to see them.

Lisette turned onto the first opening in the field, a bumpy road of loose sand and stone. The men stepped aside to let her pass. The landscape was green and flat but for the hills. She came to the end of the road where it disappeared into a field of sugarcane. And in the next minute, Lisette was pressing her tongue to the roof of her mouth, determined not to cry, not now, not over something so stupid as the colors of afternoon. She got out and stood for a moment wondering if it wasn't too late to drive to Varadero. Get a room on the beach, come back in the morning.

She looked at the sky. It had cleared and the air seemed cooler by the cane. She got in the car and sat for a while. She was hungry and tired, not herself. She turned the car around and drove slowly back the way she'd come. When she came upon the field men, she drove beside them for a while until they got off the road to let her pass. But she stopped the car and rolled down the window. She didn't give them a chance to address her in English.

"Buenas tardes," she said.

The men looked at one another, then nodded.

She asked if they knew of the old Aruna house.

"Aruna?"

The men discussed it. The man she had addressed laid down his machete and came to her window. "Santo's granddaughter?"

Lisette thought for a moment and then motioned to him to get closer as she stepped out of the car. She nodded. "Mabella's daughter."

The man's eyes narrowed before he turned to face the others.

"Oye, la hija de Mabi."

When he turned back to her, he was smiling. He took her hands. "I knew it, I knew it when I saw you, the same eyes."

"Lisidro Padron," he said, holding out his hand. "El carpintero. Your mother has told you about me probably?"

The other men crowded around her before she could disappoint Lisidro. Questions. Where were they? How were they? Any sisters? Are the old Arunas still alive? Lisette shook her head to the last one. Died in Venezuela a few years after the revolution. The man bent his head. He motioned back to his friends. "I'll take you to the house."

He paused and looked at Lisette, deciding something. "El viejo Matún and his wife are living there." Lisette shook her head like a question. "You don't know Matún and Alicia? They worked for your grandparents all their lives, since they were children almost. Matún was the only man who could grow roses in Cuba." Lisette raised her head and looked at Lisidro. After a moment she said, "Yes, of course, the roses."

Twice in the walk to the house, she tried to ask Lisidro something, a question about the winds this time of year, where the road emptied. But he walked on without turning, as if he hadn't heard her or thought her poorly bred for disturbing the silence this way. Their footsteps loosened the top thin layer of dirt on the road and sent up clouds of red-brown dust behind them. The royal palms had thinned and in between them, by the edge of the road, pink flowers grew, their petals curled under where they were beginning to brown. The air was still, the thin white clouds high in the sky, and Lisette thought again how much she often preferred the journey to the destination. Even when she was a girl and they made the long drives to visit her father's parents in Tampa, she had reveled in the passing trucks, the outposts of life, the burger joints and the dried-fruit stands, most of them gone now, the road long since widened. But those early mornings with the stars still out, she used to sit in the back and wish they would never get there, that their whole life could become this car trip. She felt it now, comfortable in her stride behind Lisidro, accustomed to the silence, not caring anymore where the road ended.

Lisidro stopped suddenly ahead of her. He turned back and waved his arm for her to hurry. He stood in front of a little iron gate painted white. He shouted into a tangle of trees and plants. Lisette came up beside him. A slender stone path led from the gate into the garden. Out of the foliage, as Lisette stood watching, came a short woman, bent over, her head covered in a black shawl. She came up to the gate, resting a brown hand on the latch, and looked into Lisette's eyes.

"La nieta de Aruna," Lisidro said. "Lisette, this is Alicia. She and Matún have been here. Have been taking care of things."

Alicia watched Lisette. Her eyes were dark brown, almost black. As Lisette watched, the woman's eyes filled with tears.

"Yes, I see the resemblance," she said.

Alicia's eyes shifted down and a tear fell slowly along her nose. Lisette put her hand over the woman's hand, like rough paper and dry as the road. Alicia turned to Lisidro and back again. She removed her hand from under Lisette's abruptly and wiped the corners of her eyes with the shawl.

"You are here to take the house."

The hardness of the woman's words startled Lisette. She looked from Lisidro to Alicia and brought her arms to her chest.

"I swear to you it's not that at all," Lisette said. "Never."

Lisidro put a hand on her shoulder and motioned with the other to go through the gate.

"La Señorita Aruna has no such intentions. She only wants to see the house. And then she'll leave."

Lisette nodded and looked back to Alicia, whose hand had come to rest on the latch again.

"The resemblance. It's quite striking," Alicia said. "Igualita."

Lisidro had to give her a small shove to get them through the gate.

When they came to the garden, the first thing Lisette saw was a rooster and then the dry dusty ground that it pecked and then a speckle of sunlight like a pebble and beyond it, above it, in a weak shadow, the house.

The house, the idea of her mother's house there in the shadow, is a present thought in this retelling, the way she described it to herself much later. Back then, standing next to Lisidro and Alicia, Lisette saw that it was a house, but it could not be the house she had come all this way to see. This was a house with small windows carved high on the uneven walls. A flat, pitted roof of red tile. A single front door, wooden and cracked. An iron latch that hung open. A house with small windows. Uneven walls. Red tiles. Iron latches. The house of someone else's imaginings, a different story. Beyond the house stood the blue hills and Cuba green and unknown, the way the first Spaniards must have seen it before they brought their straight rows of cane, tamed the wild green with double stands of palms.

Lisette saw the way Lisidro bent his head toward this house, this little dream. His lips moved, wordless. Alicia took her hand. And then Lisette was sitting at a wood table inside a small kitchen. A kerosene stove, a bucket of oil, a yellowed basin filled with water, a refrigerator covered in silver tape, black at the edges. Lisidro kept moving his lips at Lisette. She blinked. Was that her laughter? Inside it was dark; the contrast with the outdoors made her eyes hurt. She tried to look at Alicia, her polished coconut face.

Then a small door from the back of the kitchen opened and in it stood a man, naked to the waist. He carried a black bucket of dimpled fruit. When he saw the stranger at the table, he put the bucket down. Lisidro moved his lips. The man threw his arms in the air. He picked Lisette out of the chair and hugged her.

He went back to the fruit and put the bucket on the table. He picked out two pieces and laid them on a sheet of newspaper. Lisette stared at the fruit. The man finally took one in his hand and split the skin with his fingernail. The fruit smelled like roses. Lisette hesitated. The others watched her. She bit, the taste gritty and sweet, nothing like the sticky red paste that was the only thing she had known of guava in Miami. She swallowed and looked up at the man. His lips moved. And the air came rushing back.

"Your mother tell you about the guava trees here?" he said, and Lisette hearing for the first time. "Biggest fruit in all of Cuba."

Matún sat down at the last chair and pulled it up close to Lisette.

"Oye, you okay?"

He turned to his wife.

"Oye, Alicia, tráele un baso de agua."

"No, no," Lisette said. "I don't need water. I'm okay."

"You're red. This heat."

"I'm okay. Thank you."

Lisette swallowed. Matún shook a guava at her slowly.

"Tu mamá," he began. Then shook his head. "I can't believe you're here. I always used to tell my wife, it's only a matter of time before Santo's people show up again. Ay. What a wonderful thing, eh?"

He stood and walked back to a small room. Alicia and Lisidro stayed behind at the table. Lisette closed her eyes to shut out the truth that sat with its arms crossed in front of her. And what of it! she wanted to shout. So she lied for years. So she lied! If only Lisette could get up now and return to the hotel in

Havana, the men dancing on the Malecón, back to the Cuba she could talk about later, the simple stories of the rafters, the plain facts of their sadness.

"Are you comfortable?" Alicia asked.

Lisette opened her eyes and nodded. "Sí, gracias."

Matún returned with a small wooden picture frame. He handed it to Lisette. A little girl in pigtails sitting in that very kitchen, all the furniture the same, a bucket of guava in front of her.

"Tu mamá," Matún said. He shook his head, smiling.

"Your grandparents loved this house," Alicia said.

"We've tried to keep it up for them," Matún said. "Of course"—he waved his hands—"old age gets us all!" He laughed.

"Speaking of viejos—"

Lisidro stopped him. "Los viejos murieron en Venezuela."

"Ah. So sorry about your grandparents." Matún wiped his hands over his chest. "Now, you see, that makes me very sad to hear. They loved this house." Matún folded his hands. He was lost for a few seconds in contemplation. Lisidro cleared his throat. Were they waiting for Lisette to speak? She was afraid she might shout if she tried.

Matún sighed. "Of course, we didn't live here then. We lived out back." He pointed toward the window, past the empty yard. "It was a small house, ours was, nothing like this. I finally had to tear it down to build the chicken coop. You saw the roosters? Prize-winning. Back when they gave out prizes." Matún laughed again.

They were silent.

"Yes, your grandparents were very good people. There was never any problem because of"—he paused and rubbed his skin—"you know. Not with them. They'd make coffee here and holler out the back for us to come and sit with them. They had no problems that way." Alicia looked at him and then at her hands, folded on the table.

Lisette handed Matún the photograph.

"Same with us," Matún said, taking back the frame. "We'd make coffee, we'd call them over, we'd all sit together. We had no problems either. In some ways, it was better then." He looked at Lisidro and stopped. "We're just here taking care of the house. If you ever wanted to return—"

Lisette shook her head. "First time," she began. "What I mean is, if this is my first time here, how could I return?"

She looked around the table and thought to smile. Finally, Alicia laughed and they all joined in. Alicia took Lisette by the hand.

"Come, I'll show you the rest."

Lisette paused. She could see from where she sat that the rest was another small room with a chair and beyond that a room that she guessed to be where Matún and Alicia slept.

"No, gracias." Lisette pulled her hand out of Alicia's and patted her shoulder. "Later—I'll see it for the next time."

"You can't come all this way and not see the house!" Matún shouted.

"It's okay," Alicia said, looking at Lisette. "She's tired."

"Yes, I'm enough tired from the trip."

"Nonsense!"

Matún took her by the hand.

"One minute only."

Lisette stood and nodded. She let her hand relax in Matún's.

The narrow hallway that ran from the kitchen connected a small sitting room to two back rooms, each painted green.

"Your mother slept here," Matún said with a flourish of his arm.

A lace curtain covered the top half of the window, darkening the room. A wooden dresser was pushed up against the corner, its knobs worn black and shiny. The narrow bed was straight and tidy under the window.

Matún followed her gaze and nodded.

"Everything here was hers."

The others walked out and Lisette stood for a moment at the door. She walked into the room, half hearing Matún, not seeing the small rug, the low double bed, the flowered curtain strung across one corner.

She turned and walked out, following a crack in the floorboards. Lisidro and Alicia sat in two rocking chairs. A broom leaned against the door.

"My mother—" Lisette began, then stopped. She turned toward the door. When she turned back, she could feel the heat in her cheeks.

"My husband would have been so pleased to see this," she said. "It's too bad." She folded her hands and said more to herself, "My husband, Erminio."

She let his name hang in the air. Alicia and Lisidro looked at one another, but no one spoke. Lisette breathed in and smiled. She took Matún's hands and kissed him on both cheeks.

"Gracias," she said. "I must go. I have much work."

Matún kissed her. Then he put his hands behind his back and turned his head to look out the small window as he spoke.

"You know. The government has been very helpful to us. Yes, very generous with us. They gave us this land when your grandparents left. Every Sunday, me and the wife drive the scooter to Havana and sell guavas and mangoes. We are not poor; we are doing very well," he said. "Thanks to our government and the grace of God."

Alicia pulled her shawl closer. The silence of the countryside was like a weight. Lisette looked from Alicia to Matún. He was nodding to himself. "Thanks to the grace of God."

Lisette reached into her purse as if she were looking for her map. Then she took Matún's hands. She pressed the bill.

"Un regalito," she whispered.

His eyes never changed expression until he closed them and bowed ever so slightly. Gratitude and reproach, the small space between knowing and forgetting.

~

Lisette walked through the hallways, dragging one piece of furniture after another. She didn't know what she was doing. She needed to do something. And so she moved the armchair into the family room, the bar stools out to the pool. She stood and remembered the lights her father had strung all those years ago, that Christmas when the women loved Erminio. The gazebo was shabby now, a vein of mold running down one column. The lawn had grown over the flowers. It was as if the house had declined in sympathy with her father. In the last days of his illness, the Coral Gables code-enforcement board had sent them a complaint about the tall grass. Lisette had run two red lights in her anger. At city hall, she had ranted about the rights of man until a security guard escorted her out. She had regretted it and written a letter of apology later, a very proper repentance. She was an editor at the paper now, had her own office overlooking the bay. She was a little in love with a German psychologist who loved her back. In the evenings they had long conversations about the will and happiness. On Sundays, they had some people from his practice for lunch and she put out her good crystal and the leather-bound Rilke.

When, alone with him, the people gone home, she would complain of despair, her sick parents, he would hold her face and tenderly ask, "Why do you not kill yourself?"

It was an old joke with them. And Lisette always laughed. Logotherapy, he called it the first time. And she'd understood loco therapy. There is meaning in this, he insisted. And he waved his arms, meaning everything. Yes, she'd said, it's all loco.

Lisette stopped at the door to her old room. She walked to the closet. From the top shelf she pulled down a box and sat on the bed. It was the kind of box young women keep and she hadn't opened it since her last weeks in college. A graduation program sat on the top, yellowed and brittle and almost twenty years old. Bits of the foil that condoms came wrapped in. A dried corsage from her junior prom. A translucent pink cocktail stirrer whose origins had long ago disappeared into her memory. Below, near the bottom, a pink diary with a lock and a stack of photographs tight in a rubber band. Lisette winced. Had this been her life?

She sifted through the letters, names she'd forgotten, dates and places. She stopped, reached to her chest for her glasses. Love letters. Letters from friends. One note on linen paper which she opened, the paper crackling back into the present.

> L.:
> So happy you've finally decided to write that novel. I think the Cuban experience is a great idea for a book. You have to promise me one thing: You have to make fun of them. There's no other way to write this. Send me what you have.
>> Love you. Miss you. Can't wait to see you.
>> A.

The letter was typed, as if the sender wanted to remove the last trace of himself. She couldn't remember receiving it. Who was A.? Had she ever thought of writing a novel? She remembered writers she'd known in college, students, a man who had followed her for days. Was it the editor who had told her she had Great Potential? A lover? A prankster? Her ex-husband?

Had she written the note herself? She sat at her old bed and tried to reach back into the years. She met herself going the other way. Promising she would never write, never publish, never be a special section in the bookstore. Better to write about berms and set-asides, last night's vote in a small room of microphones and lights.

She took a pencil from the box. She read the letter again and folded it in half. She stared for a moment at her hand. And then she began to write:

> Beautiful Coral Gables home, five bedrooms, three
> baths, vaulted ceilings in the dining room. Balcony
> with wrought-iron railings overlooking large pool.
> Entrance flanked by royal palms.

She paused and added, The house of your dreams.

Outside by the gazebo, she slipped the letter into her pocket. She stood still to hear a peacock send its melancholy wail through the yard. A car passed the house slowly, its engine low and hungry. Tomorrow she would air the house out and the next day she would call the realtor, tell her she was in a hurry. She walked up the creaking wood steps and sat on the railing, looking out over the fraying yard. Her parents had thrown a party here after she'd returned from Cuba, all of them healthy and young, the orange trees in blossom, her cousin's daughters splashing in the pool. She'd looked up at the house, the palms framed against the sky.

What was it like? What was the house like? The children's laughter like punctuation marks.

Only her mother was silent. She sat across from her, her hands in her lap. Lisette followed her gaze. The day was bright, shimmering above the water. Lisette spoke slowly. It was too bad, she began, that the soldier had taken her camera. There was so much to see. The road to the house that crossed a wooden bridge into a field of sugarcane. The narrow path flanked on both sides by royal palms. It was a late afternoon in summer and the men were coming in from the fields, their hats flopping softly in the breeze.

But the house. What about the house?

Lisette paused, making a circle with her arms. She looked at her mother. Watched her hands turn in her lap.

"Everything was the same," Lisette said after a moment. "The stairway, the balconies. Even the marble fireplace. Somehow, it all made it through the revolution."

She faced her mother. Held her chin in her hands.

"And the long white-shuttered windows that looked over the rose garden still let in the very brightest sunshine."

The children had stopped by the edge of the pool to listen. One by one they moved away to resume their game. Her father let his gaze fall. Lisette's mother looked up. She stood and Lisette watched her go. Her cousin came out with the guitar. The chatter of the afternoon resumed. Someone passed by and patted her on the head.

Lisette closed her eyes. The guitar played a slow bolero and Lisette remembered Erminio, his Sunday poems; she saw him again against the light, pouring her morning coffee. He had wrapped his arms around her tight, held her steady against the day.

Acknowledgments

I would like to especially thank my sister Rose, my best friend and reader. Thanks to my uncle Dionisio Martínez for inspiration and example. Many thanks to the people at the NYU graduate creative writing program, especially Melissa Hammerle who has created a warm and intelligent environment for young writers. Thanks to *The New York Times* Company Foundation for their support. Thanks to Breyten Breytenbach for your guidance and wisdom. Thanks also to Adrienne Brodeur, Samantha Schnee, Rebecca Allen and Edna O'Brien. I owe so much to my agent Amy Williams for all your hard work and endless energy and to Elisabeth Schmitz at Grove/Atlantic for your unflappable good judgment.